Teddycats

RAZORBILL

An Imprint of Penguin Random House
Penguin.com

Copyright © 2016 Penguin Random House LLC

Names: Storey, Mike, 1982–
Title: Teddycats / by Mike Storey.
Description: New York City : Razorbill, 2016. | Summary: When one young Teddycat's selfish decision exposes his whole jungle community, he risks everything to save those he loves.
Identifiers: LCCN 2016026063 | ISBN 9781101998830
Subjects: | CYAC: Imaginary creatures—Fiction. | Animals—Fiction. | Rescues—Fiction. | Jungles—Fiction.
Classification: LCC PZ7.1.S756 Te 2016 | DDC [Fic]—dc23
LC record available at https://lccn.loc.gov/2016026063

Paperback ISBN 9781101998960

Printed in the United States of America

1 3 5 7 9 10 8 6 4 2

Book design by Corina Lupp

Teddycats

MIKE STOREY

RAZORBILL

An Imprint of Penguin Random House

Chapter

CLOUD KINGDOM, HOME to the Teddycats, was wedged between two dormant volcanoes in the middle of the jungle. Over the millennia, lava spillover had created a wide, smooth splash basin surrounded by insurmountable cliffs.

Well, almost insurmountable.

The Teddycats, with their long, razor-sharp claws, were one of the few species on the planet—and the only species in this particular jungle—that were specially equipped to scale the inverted rock faces that plunged down into the forest. Besides the steepness, there were other obstacles as well. For instance, the lava had hardened in unpredictable and slippery ways, ranging from the glassy to craggy; the altitude could induce anything from shortness of breath to full-on vertigo; and the heavy cloud coverage restricted visibility to near zero. While the Kingdom itself was extremely friendly—even nurturing—to all forms of life, it was not uncommon for Teddycat scouts to discover fledgling trespassers on the far outskirts, either wounded from the climb or driven mad by exhaustion.

But inside the Kingdom, all was verdant and fertile. Fresh water trickled reliably down the peaks, and bright, polished sunlight encouraged bountiful gardens and lush vegetation. Fruit trees and passionflowers clogged the well-tended Teddycat trails, and orchids and monkey brush clung in bunches to the Wall that enclosed their rarefied domain.

On his way to visit his mother at the Sanctuary, a young Teddycat named Bill Garra took comfort in the sweet sunbeams as a warm breeze brushed his fur. The Sanctuary was where ill or injured animals, all of them approved and admitted by the Teddycat Elders, could rest and recuperate in the safety and seclusion of the Kingdom. Bill's mother, Marisol, worked there most afternoons. Bill was supposed to meet his friend Luke Selva down on the forest floor, but he found himself delaying his departure.

Luke had always been curious about Cloud Kingdom, but lately he'd become increasingly adamant about visiting. And Bill was running out of excuses. He'd already blamed the rigors of the sweetmoss harvest, renovations to the Garra family den, and two separate Blood Moons. Bill wasn't sure how much longer he could keep on putting off his friend, while still being able to call himself a friend.

Because it wasn't just geology and evolution that kept Cloud Kingdom secured. The Elder Teddycats, which included Bill's father, Big Bill, were responsible for enforcing many strict rules that kept Cloud Kingdom separate from the rest of the jungle. The Teddycats' home was beautiful and rare, but accompanying all of that was a seething preoccupation with security and an undercurrent of constant fear.

Cloud Kingdom was a fiercely guarded paradise.

But Bill had never understood what the big deal was. Luke was a friend. Bill had been welcomed into Luke's den a million times. But Luke was not a Teddycat. He was an Olingo, who lived amid the raw chaos of the jungle. He couldn't be expected to understand Bill's position, let alone the rules of Cloud Kingdom.

In fact, the two of them shouldn't have had so much as two words to rub together. But Luke was the one who saved Bill from a viper bite he'd received on one of his illicit trips to the jungle floor, and they became fast buds.

Now they were in the midst of a big building project: a fort in a grand tree that had been split down the middle in a lightning storm. Bill was anxious to get down there and get back to work, but first he wanted to check and make sure his mother would be too busy to notice his absence for the rest of the afternoon.

Bill wouldn't normally have taken such careful measures, but the whole Kingdom was a bit on edge of late. Everyone was fretting about what happened to Sebastian, a Teddycat whom the Elders had recently banished from Cloud Kingdom. Right after the decision was made, a veteran scout named Diego escorted him, blindfolded, down to a remote part of the jungle, and had let him loose in the middle of nowhere, warning him never to return. Bill wasn't exactly sure of the nature of Sebastian's violation—the adults spoke of it only in whispers—but it must have been something very, very bad. Something almost . . . unimaginable. Bill had never really liked Sebastian, who always had a nasty smirk on his face and seemed to enjoy telling scary stories to young Teddycats, but he wouldn't wish banishment on anyone. Banishment from the Kingdom was the harshest punishment a Teddycat could receive. Everyone knew the jungle was a dangerous place, especially for Teddycats.

As Bill navigated the Sanctuary he spied his mother amid the friendly bustle, tending to the wounds of a hobbled—but still intimidating—jaguar. The Sanctuary's admission process was mysterious and based, as far as Bill could tell, solely on the Elders' ever-shifting whims. Mrs. Garra always described it as a delicate balancing act between helping as many souls as possible and keeping the Kingdom a secret—and the Teddycats safe.

As Bill watched his mother with the jaguar, he stroked his ear thoughtfully. How simple it was for that big old cat to come up for a stay in Cloud Kingdom. Why couldn't Luke come down with some minor, easily curable ailment? Then Bill could ask his parents if he could nominate him for the Sanctuary, Luke would get a look at the Kingdom, and everybody would be happy.

His ear went numb with a pinch of realization. Even if Luke *were* to get sick and come to the Sanctuary, it wouldn't take long for everyone to figure out that Luke and Bill were friends, and that Bill had regularly been sneaking out of Cloud Kingdom—another major

Teddycat no-no. His thoughts turned again to Sebastian, all alone out there in the wild. Whatever he had done, surely it was much, much worse than sneaking down to the jungle or bringing a good friend up to Cloud Kingdom.

Bill craned his neck to get a better look at his mother pressing leaves and balm against the jaguar's wounds. This was a rare opportunity to safely observe one of the jungle's fiercest predators. While Bill wanted nothing more than to tell Luke about the jaguar—Luke would absolutely flip at the idea of an up-close look at a docile jungle cat—it would only intensify his demands to visit. Bill sighed. After one last look at the cat he made his way to the Wall.

AS BILL DESCENDED into the leafy canopy, his heart began to beat at a different rate. The forest floor held an energy he craved. In some ways it suited him better than home, and no amount of stern warnings had kept him away. He swung from vine to vine, limb to limb. Crystals of dew collected on his fur, and his eyes watered from wind and joy.

Today was the day Bill was supposed to take the loose fronds and downed limbs Luke had been collecting, and cut and fashion them into tools and supplies with his claws. And here was yet another violation of Teddycat regulations. Cloud Kingdom security was a big deal, but claws—the things that got the Teddycats up into the lofty branches in the sky in the first place—were an even bigger one. The Teddycats' claws were to be used only for clearly defined situations of basic survival, such as hunting and gathering and securing shelter. Brandishing a single claw for anything other than a life-or-death situation could get a Teddycat in serious trouble—maybe even banishment.

Bill knew the Elders had good reasons rooted in Teddycat history to make these rules, but he still often wondered why they were so intent on controlling their subjects. He personally felt Teddycats should be free to use their claws however they saw fit, and he figured that while he was down in the jungle, the rules didn't apply.

He arrived at the fort to find Luke already there, arranging the fronds and limbs. Bill apologized for his lateness, and the two quietly set to work.

The fort was coming along nicely. They had been working on it for months. It would serve as a home away from home, a hideout, a place to relax away from the restrictions of the Kingdom. In many ways, Luke was the ideal partner. He worked largely without complaint, listened when Bill needed to vent about his parents or the Elders, and indulged Bill's more harebrained dreams and schemes. But today Luke had been bristling from the moment Bill had arrived, and Bill had no doubt that it had to do with his frustrations about Cloud Kingdom.

They were digging for stones, and then lugging them over to the creek. The idea was to plug the stream, which would eventually swell into a combination swimming hole and protective moat. The stones clacked, rolled, and settled as the two grunted in the stifling humidity.

"Hey, Bill?" ventured Luke, and Bill bit his lip, awaiting the inevitable.

"Yeah?" Bill asked. He scratched his head with his claw, a bad habit, but one he often lapsed into in the jungle.

"Well," Luke said, "I've pretty much shown you everything there is to see in the jungle, wouldn't you agree?"

"You've been a top-shelf ambassador, Luke," Bill said. "There's no denying that."

Since the very first day they met, Luke had always been willing to show Bill the forest in all of its chaotic glory. The everyday dangers of gathering places and hunting grounds, secret paths and cooling pools. They swiped colorful feathers from high nests, collected fruit, traded plans for the future as frogs serenaded them from the trees.

"But I'm still left wondering," Luke said, slowly, "when are you going to return the favor? You keep saying you're going to show me Cloud Kingdom, but there's always some reason or another why you can't."

"What's mine is yours," Bill said, pointing to the thatched roof of the fort. "You know that."

"This has nothing to do with the fort," Luke said. "I'm talking about real life. I've introduced you to my family. You've been a guest in my home. I'm proud to call you a friend!"

"Yeah, and I love Doris and Freddy Selva and all the Olingos!" Bill said, growing very uneasy now. "So what's wrong?"

"Your whole life is a secret! All I know about your home and your family is what you accidentally let slip, usually while you're complaining about the Elders. But I have no idea where you lay your head down at night. I can't even imagine it, and that's not fair."

Luke plopped down in the creek. Water beaded on his fur, and he seemed to expand with disappointment.

"Listen, Luke," Bill said, having no choice but to speak frankly, "there are things about me, details about Cloud Kingdom, that I just can't get into, no matter how badly I want to share them with you."

"I know," said Luke, rolling his eyes. "But at a certain point you have to decide whether or not you trust me. That's what friends do, Bill."

Sometimes Bill felt like he was always playing two sides, leaving everybody miffed. "Believe me, I wish things were different."

The Olingos and Teddycats had once been fierce allies. They were similar in appearance (the Olingos were a bit clumsier, with duller claws and grayer fur), and had complementary skills. But when the Teddycats moved to Cloud Kingdom, they left the Olingos behind to fend for themselves. And the Olingos never forgave them. Historically, the Teddycats—the colder, more pragmatic of the two species—treated this rift and the pain and guilt it caused as just part of the price they paid for safety. After all, they had to look out for themselves.

But if anyone ever bothered to ask what an Olingo thought of the Teddycats, he would likely describe them as selfish cowards. A Teddycat, on the other hand, might say the Olingos lacked conviction and discipline. The truth was, they were stronger together (as Bill had discovered through his friendship with Luke), but it was hard to imagine them joining forces again.

"If you really wanted things to be different, you'd take me up there with you," Luke said.

"I can't!" yelled Bill. "I'm sorry. I know I said I would, I know I keep stalling and telling you that someday we'll be able to go. But the truth is, you aren't allowed in Cloud Kingdom, and I'm not allowed to take you. That's one thing I can't do, so please, just drop it."

Luke turned away. Bill immediately regretted his outburst.

"Anyways," Bill said, trying to salvage the day—and his friendship, "the swimming hole is really coming along. I bet by tomorrow we'll be doing backflips and belly flops!"

"I'm busy tomorrow," Luke huffed.

Bill closed his eyes. Sounds of the wild filled his head. Creaking fronds, swaying vines, the hum of insects and birds, the darting tongues of creatures in the trees. His eyelids turned pink with the sunlight slanting through the canopy at a disturbing angle. His eyes snapped open. He had lost track of the time.

"Uh-oh," Bill said. "I'm really sorry, Luke, but I have to head back."

"I guess it's true what they say about Teddycats," Luke said.

"What's that?" Bill asked, already wincing.

"They only care about themselves."

BILL STARTED BACK to Cloud Kingdom, distracted by his thoughts. Why, exactly, *couldn't* he bring Luke home? What ever happened to goodwill, hospitality, the importance of caring for friends in low places? There was no doubt in Bill's mind that Cloud Kingdom would be a better place if the Elders loosened the borders a little. He didn't share their panic at the mere thought. To them, every intruder was a threat; every stranger just an enemy they hadn't yet encountered.

Outsiders like Luke didn't understand, but that wasn't their fault. They weren't meant to understand. Luke hadn't grown up with the rules of Cloud Kingdom drilled into his brain at every opportunity: the importance of secrecy as the first line of defense, the society as a closed system, the damning indictment of all outsiders. And the Elders would say that the less he knew the better.

But from Luke's perspective, his exclusion from the Kingdom was Bill's personal choice. Well, whatever the real reasons behind keeping Luke out of Cloud Kingdom, Bill didn't want to be that kind of friend. And he certainly didn't want Luke to think of him the way he did about Teddycats in general.

The air began to cool as Bill entered the blanket of fog that settled above the jungle canopy, at the foot of Cloud Kingdom. There were ways to sneak Luke past the sentries who guarded the entrance, and it happened to be an especially convenient time to do so. The Elders were busy discussing the High Council nominations, and his parents were either with the Elders or otherwise preoccupied with Big Bill's career.

Bill thought back to Luke's sad eyes, the way they had drooped with disappointment when Bill left him floating by the fort. He sighed. Might as well try and fit one last caper in before suppertime.

He swiftly descended out of the fog and back into the jungle.

Chapter

LUKE GRIPPED TIGHTLY to the fur of Bill's back.
The journey up to Cloud Kingdom was disorienting and counterintuitive. North twisted to south; west
whisked to the east. Bill was careful to stick to back
channels as he ripped up the thin, roughly hewn path.
Luke's breath was encouraging, brisk and steady in his
ear, but as landmarks began to appear—the final gasp
of the tree line, the chill of the fog—Bill grew more and
more apprehensive. He imagined a familiar look of disappointment dawning on his mother's face. The stitch
of doubt in the back of his mind frayed a bit further, but
Bill was moving too quickly to stop.

They broke through the Wind Tunnel and slipped behind the waterfall. This was the final climb. Just above them lay Cloud Kingdom, a square klick of green, fertile land wrapped in billowy vapor.

Bill's plan, sketchy as it was, had them high-tailing it to a protected, shaggy vantage point overlooking the Sanctuary. Luke could get a good look at the jaguar, then they'd zoom over to his friend Maia Pata's den, which was on the outer ring of the Kingdom, conveniently close to their probable exit point. Bill knew Maia would be home. She always left school early to care for her younger sister, Elena. Bill hoped he could give Luke a quick tour, and then get him out of there before any Elder was the wiser. If anyone in the Sanctuary asked any questions, he could always pass Luke off as a patient.

Bill cleared the cloud cloak, vaulted over the Wall, and began the gentle slide into the basin. He heard Luke gasp at the sight before them, and for a moment Bill's nerves succumbed to a swell of pride. The sky was a brilliant blue, as if the clouds had scrubbed it clean. This same clarity extended to the air, which was dry yet sweet enough to gulp, and the cold, clear water, which trickled through the Kingdom with its reassuring babble. When the first Teddycats arrived at Cloud Kingdom they divided it into an irrigated grid, allowing nearly every den—even those in the far reaches, in the shadow of the peaks—access to drinking water and fertile land.

"It's beautiful," said Luke, obviously awed.

"Just remember," Bill said, "it's all about discretion and keeping a low profile. And if anyone asks, you're seriously sick."

Luke crouched down and practiced the fake cough Bill had taught him, but it sounded more like a sneezing snort than a serious respiratory ailment. Bill sighed. It would have to do.

They bolted down the lane toward the Sanctuary, swerving behind blossom-choked shrubbery and clinging to the shadows. As they crouched against an abandoned den, waiting for a near-blind Elder to hobble past, Bill heard the unmistakable, creaking shift of an Elder disturbed. He froze and gestured for Luke to do the same.

"Is this the Sanctuary?" Luke asked.

Bill grimaced, and indicated for Luke to hush. Suddenly, there was a new shadow. And it definitely didn't belong to an Elder, or even another Teddycat. The head of the wizened jaguar emerged quizzically from the den Bill had assumed was abandoned. Marisol must have rubbed him down with salve and stashed him here to rest. The jaguar's rich, spotted fur was speckled with gray, and his eyes were kind and milky.

"S-sorry," Bill said. "I didn't realize this den was occupied."

The jaguar smiled a toothy grin. "And who is your friend?"

His voice was rough yet warm. Bill had expected something a bit more sinister.

"Who, me?" Luke said, clearly still adjusting to his surroundings. "Oh, I'm sick." He fake-coughed twice for good measure.

Bill willed his friend quiet with a bug-eyed glare.

The jaguar glanced up and down the empty lane. "Well, it seems as if you're in a hurry. You'd better run along." And then, to Luke: "I hope you feel better soon."

Bill did a lightning-quick double take, then darted off, Luke in tow. He had been expecting more of a tongue-lashing, though they weren't in the clear just yet.

"Thank you!" cried Luke as they scurried away.

THEY ALL BUT slid into the Pata family den, panting and kicking up dust. She was huddled over Elena, settling the little Teddycat down for a nap in a plump pile of straw. But as soon as Maia stood up, Elena did too, and the straw flew everywhere. Maia growled in frustration, but Elena was oblivious, rushing to greet Bill.

"Bill!" she screeched, flinging herself on his leg with wild abandon.

"Howdy, Elena," said Bill, flattered by the attention but sorry to have made things more difficult for Maia. "Hi, Maia," he said, looking up at her apologetically.

"Well, look what the Teddycat dragged in," Maia said.

Maia and Bill had grown up in adjacent dens, and many of Bill's first memories were of the two of them together. Despite her family's move, they remained close, in part because Maia, though seemingly straight-laced and unquestionably responsible—she basically raised Elena on her own after their mother became sick—was actually kind of a rebel. For instance, she gave nonsanctioned furcuts in the Crook after lessons, styling their friends' fur with nutrient-rich sap she mined from trees. She was especially good at carving designs into the fur above the ears with an illicit flick of her claw. She was wiry and compact, smart and fun, with a quizzical coolness to her eyes and a mischievous lilt to her snout.

Bill knew he was very lucky to count her as a friend.

"Who's this?" her little sister, Elena, asked, looking at Luke with a touch of her old shyness.

"This here is Luke. He's an Olingo. From the jungle. He's not feeling so hot, so he came up here to get some treatment."

"Wow," said Elena, with a mixture of excitement and pity.

"Hey, Maia, what do you know about your new neighbor?" Bill asked, referring to the jaguar. He was trying to shift the attention from Luke, but after his unexpected interaction with the injured cat, he found himself strangely curious.

"Hmm?" Maia said.

"You know, the elderly jaguar currently residing four dens down the lane?"

"That's Felix!" said Elena. "He got bit by a human."

"Almost," said Maia. "But not quite, sweetie. He got snared in a human trap."

"Lousy Joe," said Bill, punching a paw.

Joe was the name the Teddycats gave the human who stalked the innocent animals of the jungle. He was a wily, hulking monster, accompanied by a sharp stench and a smoking stick clenched between his glinting gold teeth.

"How badly is he hurt?" Bill asked.

"What am I, a doctor? Ask your mom. But I'd guess it must be pretty bad if they let him up here." Maia turned away from Luke and her sister and tapped Bill on the shoulder. "Hey, Bill, can I talk to you for a minute?"

"You bet!" said Bill, smiling but unmoving.

There was an awkward beat.

"Um, privately?" Maia said.

Privacy was hard to come by in Cloud Kingdom. With its active citizenry and geographical restrictions, there was little room to hide. Whispers carried. Bill had been back on the grounds only for five minutes and already he had run into a convalescing jungle cat, not to mention Elena, whom Bill considered friendly but too young to be trusted with sensitive information. The privacy situation went a long way in explaining the appeal of the fort, which, ironically, had so far led to more secrets.

Bill crossed the den, leaving the light that spilled through the entrance, and soon found himself in a dank corner. He shivered involuntarily. "What do you think you're doing?" Maia hissed, backing Bill further against the cool dirt wall, as far out of earshot as the den allowed.

"What do you mean?" Bill said.

"Don't pretend you don't know," Maia said. "That Olingo's *not* sick, and you know it."

"Oh, come on," said Bill, smiling.

But the smile seemed to make things worse. He quickly swallowed it back.

"No, *you* come on," said Maia. "I can get into seriously hot water just by having you here. Shoot, just by *seeing* the two of you and not reporting it. I know for a fact Luke isn't a sanctioned visitor. He's your friend, isn't he? The one you sneak out to go see?"

"Please, Maia. You don't need to tell anyone about this," said Bill. "Luke is a good friend. He's helped me out of some serious jams in the jungle . . ."

"Where you're not supposed to be!" Maia reminded.

"I know all that! But, Maia, he's a really good guy, and he keeps asking me where I live and why can't he see it and how it's not fair, and I got to thinking, you know, it's not entirely unreasonable for . . ."

"Clamp it," said Maia. "I have to think."

Bill did as she asked and stared down at his hind paws.

"Was there an accident? A miscommunication? Did he follow you up here? Trick you? Blackmail you? Give me something here, Garra."

"Well . . ." started Bill.

"Hey, Bill?" Elena asked, loudly, from across the den. "Is Luke an interloper?" She pronounced the word, which was often employed by the more hawkish Elders, as if it were some kind of sweet, exotic melon.

Maia pivoted. "That's not a very nice way to talk about our guest!" she said, then left Bill to rejoin Elena and Luke, where she unfurled her characteristic warmth.

Bill remained in the corner for another moment, feeling both very small and wildly out of control.

AFTER A FEW minutes of chit-chat, during which Bill and Maia were getting more and more on edge, looking over their shoulders for Elders or other potential witnesses, Bill finally decided that Luke had seen enough.

"Luke, we'd better get you back to the Sanctuary," Bill said. "You need to rest if you're going to get better."

Luke frowned but then gave Bill a wink, letting him know he understood. "It was so great to meet you, Luke," said Maia, clearing up their mild mess. "And I hope you feel better soon."

"Oh, right," he said, then coughed into his paw.

"Bye, Bill!" said Elena, refastening on his leg.

"Hey, I'll be back to see you before you know it," Bill said.

Luke jumped onto Bill's back while Elena was still attached to his leg. The three of them formed a stumbling mass too wide to fit through the den entrance. Bill gently peeled Elena off his shin and tried to say goodbye to Maia, who was deliberately avoiding his eye. His heart sank a bit as he went out the door and she shifted out of sight.

Just when Bill thought he might be able to slip out of Cloud Kingdom without any more surprises, he found one waiting for him right outside the den. It was Omar Cola, a former friend of his, just standing there with his forepaws crossed over his chest. Omar appeared smugly satisfied, as if he had just tripped over a useful secret. Bill shot up straight in surprise, leaving Luke to slide down his back and tumble into the soft grass along the lane.

"Hello, Bill," Omar said.

"Hello, Omar."

The two Teddycats entered into a staring contest as Luke struggled to collect himself.

Bill deployed a steady, narrow glare. Omar managed to work up a good sneer, but his eyes wobbled a bit, along with his chin. Omar was skinny, with ribs pressing against his coat. He was wily but unpopular, with a tendency to collect beans and spill them in front of Elders. This willingness to honk on private matters made other young Teddycats less than friendly.

No one would be able to guess it from observing this interaction, but there had been a time when the three of them—Bill, Maia, and Omar—had been inseparable. It wasn't until recently that a rift had grown between Bill and Omar. Perhaps it was because Bill was a more confident kitten than Omar. He attracted attention, for better or worse, while Omar tended to blend into his surroundings. Still, Bill didn't really know why they had stopped being friends. There had been no final fight. The two simply didn't talk for a while, and then the silence hardened, first into mistrust and then, finally, distaste.

Finally, Bill broke his gaze. What was the point? Omar had already seen Luke. "Hi, Omar," Bill said. "Long time no see."

Omar smirked. "Just what kind of trouble are you scaring up today, Bill?"

No way was Omar going to believe Luke's pathetic cough, so Bill tried quickly to come up with another story. "Meet Luke the Olingo," Bill said. "He's here on a . . . diplomacy trip. To discuss the poaching problem the Olingos are facing. I was actually just about to show him out."

Omar's eyes refocused on Luke, who put on an expression of fake fright.

"It's true," Luke said. "Those humans are out to get us."

"Admit it," Bill said. "You gotta think he'd be *especially* vulnerable."

"Maybe so," said Omar, "but I don't trust a word that comes out of your mouth."

"Doesn't make it any less true," Bill said. "Well, see you around, Omar."

And with that, Bill and Luke were off. They fled back to the Wall and down to the tree line. After a quick farewell, Luke was gone, and Bill was left to face Cloud Kingdom alone.

Dusk approached and the sky began to blend into the clouds. Bill doubled back to his den, really wishing he could start over and see a friendly face. But while his last trip had been marked by nerve-racking chance encounters, now the Kingdom felt strangely deserted. He was almost relieved to see the jaguar, Felix, this time soaking in the hot spring.

"Hello there," said Bill. "Again."

"Good evening," said Felix.

"Sorry if I woke you earlier. I'm Bill Garra. You're Felix, right?"

"I am," the jaguar said. "It's nice to formally meet you, Bill."

The water bubbled, releasing a sulfurous odor. Bill had no interest in the smelly hot spring, which was always jammed with snooty Elders. But he understood that it held restorative properties.

"Is your friend feeling better?" Felix asked.

"Yeah, I guess," said Bill. "He's home safe now. The truth is . . . well, he was never really sick to begin with."

Felix nodded, as if he already knew.

"I think," Bill said, absentmindedly scratching his head, "that I messed up pretty bad today."

"It's not fun to make mistakes," Felix said.

"You're telling me."

"But I think mistakes are inevitable. And valuable— as long as you learn from them."

"Really?" Bill said. "I guess I just don't understand why Luke can't visit. He's a loyal friend."

"The jungle is a dangerous place. It's hard, but you'll understand when you're older."

"Yeah," muttered Bill. "After I make about a million more mistakes."

Felix laughed. "Probably. But as my father always said, 'Dust yourself off and try again.'"

"My dad says, 'Mind your mother' and 'Keep your snout clean.'"

"Well, my father said those things, too."

Bill suddenly felt shy. "I should run home for dinner," he said. "Get well soon, Felix."

"Oh, you'll be rid of me in no time," Felix said. "But I wish you luck, Bill Garra."

Chapter

3

IT TOOK SOME time for Bill to fall asleep that night, but the next morning, he felt a bit better. An early fog was burning away under a gentle sun. Happy clatter and comforting smells wafted through the den. Cloud Kingdom felt less like a fortress and more like home.

His mother was already up, fixing breakfast. Bread-fruit porridge. Not a personal favorite, but not the worst recipe in her arsenal. That would be root stew, which Bill choked down only when his father was watching.

"Good morning, sunshine," Marisol said. Well, she sang it really. Ordinarily, Bill would find her singing (and her dancing, and her tendency to lapse into gibberish and flabbergasted expressions, and her kissing attacks) embarrassing, and downright deadly when she did it outside their den. But this morning her wacky ways comforted him.

"Mornin', Mom," said Bill.

"Now, I know you don't *love* my porridge," Marisol said, "but I tried to sweeten it up a bit."

"It smells great," Bill fibbed.

Marisol watched him take a lap with his dry morning tongue. Just as Bill had expected, it tasted the same as ever.

"So, what do you think?" Marisol asked.

"It's very savory," Bill said, smacking his lips and rubbing his paws together, really hamming it up.

"Okay, wise guy," said Marisol. "Take it down a notch."

"No, really!" Bill said, laughing. "It's my new ultimate all-time favorite."

"Very funny," said Marisol. "You know, there are plenty of folks out there who would go bananas for a nice homemade porridge. Down in the jungle, the way things are? Forget about it."

The porridge was gritty with nutrients. Seeds stuck in Bill's teeth.

"Bananas would be a nice touch," Bill said. "Actually, now that you mention it, Mom," he began, slowly, "why are we so separated from the jungle? I mean, I get that Cloud Kingdom's up there and the jungle's down there and all, but . . ."

"It's just the way things are, I'm afraid," Marisol said.

"But if there's suffering down there, we could do something about it."

"We do help," said Marisol. "In our way."

"Right, the Sanctuary, I know," said Bill. "I walked through there yesterday and met Felix."

"Oh, really?" Marisol said, clearly surprised that Bill was on a first-name basis with the visiting cat. "Well, there ya go. Felix is a perfect example of how the Teddycats help out in the jungle."

"Mom?" Bill asked in between bites of porridge. "I have this . . . friend. We have lessons together. And he was wondering . . . what would happen, exactly, if a Teddycat brought another species up to Cloud Kingdom?"

"You mean, like Felix?" said Marisol. "He's here with the permission of the Elders. You know that."

"Right, sure. But . . . what if another kind of animal came up here *without* permission?"

"*Without* permission?" Marisol repeated. "How would that even happen? Who is this friend asking you these wild questions?"

"I don't know, Mom! Like I said, it was just a

question," Bill said. The day was starting to feel less bright by the minute.

"Well, I can say this," Marisol said, her tone tightening. "If a Teddycat were ever to knowingly expose Cloud Kingdom, or even reveal the route to Cloud Kingdom, that would be an offense that could be punishable by banishment."

Banishment? A shiver rippled down Bill's spine.

"Even if it was just an Olingo?"

"*Especially* if it were an Olingo!" Marisol said.

Bill concentrated on his porridge, willing himself to stay calm. "But it can't be *that* big a deal, right?" he said. "I mean, it's nothing like what Sebastian did."

As soon as Bill said Sebastian's name, Marisol froze. She stopped fussing with tidying the den and stared straight at Bill. Her expression was grave and filled with concern.

"Look at me, Bill," she said.

Bill met his mother's eyes.

"This is important. Sebastian acted very selfishly. He risked the exposure of the Kingdom to dangerous elements, all to enrich himself. The resources of Cloud Kingdom—the water, the sweetmoss, the fruit—is reserved for Teddycats and the select few we believe we can safely accommodate. And bringing up an Olingo . . ."

Marisol sighed. "Many years ago, Teddycats and Olingos lived together in a place called Horizon Cove," she said.

"I know all of this, Mom," Bill said. "The story of Horizon Cove is, like, the first thing they teach us in lessons."

While Bill knew about this shared history between his kind and Luke's, the reality of it was hard to imagine. Teddycats and Olingos had been at odds for ages, since well before Bill was born, and he knew the troubles went back much further than that. But he never felt awkward when he was with Luke. There was something natural and easy about their time together. When Bill overheard other Teddycats speak about Olingos, saying they were lazy, stupid, weak, dirty, and distrustful, he didn't recognize his friend in their belittlements.

"Well, you're going to listen to this anyway," Marisol said. Her tone was gentle, but stern enough to make Bill sit up a little straighter. "Horizon Cove was a beautiful place, protected from the elements by a deep, secret ravine. But when the fierce predators closed in, the Teddycats had to make a decision: Stay and fight, or leave and find a new place to call home and raise our kittens. The Elders sent scouts, who climbed until they found Cloud Kingdom. We left the very next night."

"But I still don't understand why the Olingos didn't come along, too."

"They couldn't mobilize as quickly," Marisol said. "Or climb as high."

"So we just left them there in the Cove? They could've been wiped out!"

"The Elders have one responsibility, Bill. Survival of our kind." A hint of grief slipped into Marisol's voice now. "I know how cold that sounds, but it's just a fact of life. Cloud Kingdom has to remain a secret, Bill. There's too much at risk. We're lucky that the hunters who drove us out haven't found us here. Hopefully, they never will."

Bill's heart was beating wildly. His vision blurred. How could he have made such a horrible mistake? Had he really just put the Teddycats in danger by bringing one little Olingo up to visit?

"I don't know if hiding is the answer," said Bill. "Think of everything we sacrifice and everything we've left behind."

Marisol gave Bill a sad smile. "You're sweet, kiddo," she said. "Just promise me you'll behave. And no more talk about Sebastian. That's something for grown Teddycats to worry about."

"Fine," Bill said with a sigh.

"Now finish your breakfast."

Chapter

 4

BILL AND MAIA sat together in their meeting place in the Crook. The Crook was once just another dead branch, but it had been rescued by a network of green offshoots, which crossed and fused together, creating a thick, smooth webbing, a natural hammock overlooking a far corner of the Kingdom. But instead of the usual conversation that flowed between them—about lessons and friends and funny things their instructors and families did and said—there was only strained silence and the weight of Bill's growing guilt.

Bill took a deep breath. "I need to say something."

"Okay," Maia said, slowly.

"And I think I can say it only to you."

"Hey, you can tell me anything," Maia said. "You know that."

"Every decision I make is the wrong one, Maia."

"You're always moving at a million klicks an hour, in a million different directions, Bill," Maia said. "I can see how you might get twisted up now and then. My mom says we're just at that age."

Bill and Maia were born mere moments apart. Big Bill, who rarely reminisced, liked to tell the story of that night, the way the newborns' bleats blended together beneath a spectacular moon, waking everybody up.

"No, Maia. I might have really done it this time," Bill said.

A shiver hit him as he said it aloud.

"Bill, just tell me what's going on already," Maia said. "Nothing is going to get any easier until you do."

"Okay," Bill said. "Well, remember Luke?"

"How could I forget?"

"Well, you might have noticed that he's not a Teddycat. And I know you noticed that he wasn't sick. And, well, according to my mom, bringing him up here was a banishable offense."

"You already knew that, Bill!" Maia said.

Bill stood up and began to pace the Crook. "Sure, I knew it was *frowned* upon! And hey, you know I like to have fun and everything, but I don't know what I would do if somebody actually got *hurt* because of me."

"Slow down," Maia said. "Let's not get ahead of ourselves. Who's hurt?"

"No one! Not yet, that is. But when I brought up the topic of visitors in Cloud Kingdom, my mom got very serious very quickly," Bill said, wringing his paws. "And I wasn't exactly honest and forthcoming about why I was asking her about it."

"Marisol is an extremely smart Teddycat," said Maia. "I'm sure she knows more than you think she does. And by the way, you're not the only one around here who sometimes feels stifled by the Elders and their rules. Or by Cloud Kingdom in general."

"That's good to know," Bill said, taking genuine comfort from her words.

"I mean, we're not all as obnoxious about it as you are, maybe . . ."

"Thanks a lot," Bill said, laughing.

"Just remember, you're not in this alone," Maia said. She patted the space beside her on the smooth bough, and Bill slumped down again. "But next time you want to break a major regulation, you might want to think twice. I don't know what I'd do if you really did get banished. For starters, Elena would absolutely lose it."

Bill nuzzled against Maia's shoulder. He felt better, as he always did after talking with his friend. "Where is Elena anyways?"

"Oof, I needed a break," Maia said, stretching her arms out and yawning. Bill noticed, not for the first time, the striking streaks of color in her fur. "I left her with a little friend to play, but I know she's around here somewhere."

"Bill!"

The shrill call echoed from somewhere below. Both Maia and Bill's ears perked up, and they locked eyes.

Then, the call came again.

"Bill Garra!"

Bill's heart sank. "That sounds like Luke," he said.

"Is he in trouble?" Maia asked. "What's he doing here?"

Bill shot Maia a worried look, then bolted out of the Crook. He hustled to a little-used pathway down to the jungle. This was the express route, a straight drop. He swooped and zipped through the canopy so fast the friction shredded the vines.

Bill panted, taking in his surroundings as he rested on a low limb, just above the forest floor. There was Luke, but he didn't appear to be in any danger. On the contrary, he was surrounded by a gang of fluffy, expectant Olingo faces. These must be Luke's cousins.

He had often mentioned them—they seemed to be Luke's only other friends besides Bill—but Bill had yet to be formally introduced.

"Luke!" Bill shouted, confused and still dizzy from the drop. "What are you doing here?"

"Bill!" Luke said. "I had such a great time yesterday! I just had to bring my cousins back to see it all."

"Luke, what are you thinking? You know I broke a huge rule by bringing you up, right? I could've gotten into real trouble yesterday. Still might!"

"Sorry, Bill," Luke said, embarrassed. "We weren't meeting today, and I didn't know how else to get in touch with you."

"You shouldn't have gotten in touch at all! From now on, I'll see you when I see you, okay?" Bill reminded himself of his father. It was a strange feeling. Still, he kept going. "I thought you were in trouble! Why else would you come back here? So I double-timed it down, and now I find that not only are you perfectly fine, you've gone and blabbed about Cloud—ahem, my *home* . . . after sitting on the secret for not even one day!"

Luke sank back on his haunches, and Bill immediately felt sorry. But he couldn't just forgive and forget, right? It was better to double down and scare everyone off his scent for good.

Still, it seemed to Bill that whenever he had the chance to do the right thing for Cloud Kingdom. it didn't really *feel* like the right thing. After all, this was Luke, his partner in crime! If not for him, Bill could have been a goner, living out his last days as a lump inside of a viper. And the fort was almost done! Maybe the two of them could bring the Teddycats and the Olingos together again . . .

Bill's grim expression softened. "Listen," he said. "I'm sorry. It's just—"

A terrible, sickening *whoosh* interrupted him and rustled his fur. Bill turned just in time to see Elena, slipping through the canopy and falling, fast and hard. She landed with a thud on the forest floor, then rose, clearly dazed, and looked up. Her already wide eyes stretched further with fear and welling tears.

"Elena!" Bill hollered. "Hold on! I'm coming to get you!"

He leapt off the limb, leaving Luke and his cousins to shake and fret, and dug his claws into the tree trunk. Just as he began to scamper his way down, he heard a loud, snapping click. He snapped his gaze over to Elena. It was a trap. A human one.

And Elena had fallen directly into it.

All on its own, the large metal cage fastened shut and locked into place.

Elena gripped the wires with her tiny paws. "Bill!" she cried out. "Help me!"

Panic surged through Bill. For a moment, he couldn't even move. He was frozen, stuck on the trunk, but his thoughts were racing. *This is all my fault, Maia will never forgive me, I'll be banished, our lives are over.* Bill's heart was clenched like a fist. Then, all of a sudden, it burst open and he scrambled down to the ground.

"I've got you, Elena," Bill said, making his voice as soothing as he could manage. "Just a second here. Nothing to worry about."

Bill fumbled with the trap. He tried to fit his claw into the contraption that had clicked, thinking that was the thing keeping the entrance shut, but it wouldn't fit. He began to saw and gnaw at the wires.

"Bill" Elena whispered. "There's something coming. Behind you."

A long shadow fell over Bill and Elena. Bill watched it stretch and swell as its source crept closer. Anything with a shadow that size couldn't be entirely friendly. Even if it was a leaf-chomping herbivore, there would still be serious trouble if it came stampeding through with the two of them caught underfoot. Worst of all, maybe it was Joe, with his stolen snakeskins and furs.

Bill wanted his mother. He would even be grateful to see Big Bill Garra at his meanest, swooping down to free Elena, vanquish the shadow, and lead them back home.

The dense vegetation rustled as the presence approached. Soon it would break through the brush and it would be too late. Elena whimpered. Bill wondered how much she understood. If he stayed to fight, it was possible he could fend off the shadow and eventually unlock the cage, but it was far more likely that he would wind up wounded or worse, with nobody left to tell the Elders who had taken Elena. Just as he'd come to the conclusion that there were no good options, a vine dropped down and dangled before him.

"Hey, Bill!" hissed Luke. "Grab on!"

Bill brushed the vine aside. He knew what he had to do. He gulped, dug in, and got ready to pounce.

"Come on, Bill!" Luke whispered urgently. "What are you doing? Hurry up! That thing is headed straight for the clearing!"

"I can't do that!" Bill said. "I can't leave her down here all alone."

The brush broke open. It wasn't a stampeding herbivore. It wasn't a hungry carnivore, either. Bill had never seen it before, but he was absolutely certain what it was.

It was Joe.

Joe was the true threat to Cloud Kingdom, not Luke, not even his own big mouth. The humans were the reason for the Elders' fears and strict laws, their insistence on secrecy, the heavy cloak of silence every Teddycat was expected to wear.

Bill felt faint. He heard Elena's cries behind him. The world was quickly slipping away. Joe's face was obscured by the brim of an object perched atop its head. It began to tilt its head toward the cage, and Bill's vision began to narrow to a panicked slit.

He was about to make a desperate lunge, when Luke swooped down on the vine, knocking Bill into the brush and landing on top of him. Bill looked up just in time to watch the vile human snatch up the cage. Elena huddled in one corner, tiny and helpless.

Bill tried to call out, but Luke gripped his snout shut. His strength was surprising. Bill managed to get out a wild croaking sound, and the human froze for a moment, surveying the clearing. Bill's breath caught in his lungs. He waited, hoping he'd managed to spook it. But then the human turned back around and carried Elena off into the jungle.

Once the coast was clear, Luke released his grip on Bill, who then pushed himself away from his friend as violently as he could muster. Together they emerged from the dark brush and into a ghostly shaft of sunlight.

"I'm so sorry, Bill," Luke said, his eyes downcast.

"Don't apologize to me," Bill snarled, pushing him away. "Apologize to Elena. When we get her back."

"I will," Luke said. "I swear."

"You'd better believe it," Bill said.

Luke tried to console his friend, but they both knew there was nothing he could say. Elena was gone.

Chapter

 5

"**S**TOP BLURTING NONSENSE and just tell me what's wrong!" Maia said.

But the more Bill said, the less Maia understood.

He was out of breath and borderline hysterical, and all he could do was break the news into small, single words and let her connect them.

"Elena. Jungle. Cage. Human."

"Oh, no," Maia said. She began to shake.

"I'm so, so sorry," Bill said.

"How could this happen, Bill?" she wailed. "What did you do?"

It was the exact response he had been dreading. Maia looked like she might be sick.

"I didn't realize she had followed me down from the Crook. I didn't see her. I didn't know."

His mind buzzed with guilt and fear. He honestly couldn't recall his life before Elena fell out of the tree, that surreal moment when she slipped through his grasp and into a whole new, terrifying world. Until that moment, real disasters had been only hypothetical. Boring history lessons, gloomy warnings from Elders.

"Maia, I promise I'll do whatever it takes to get your sister back."

"You can't do anything now!" Maia said fiercely. "You've done more than enough already. We are going straight to the Elders. I'm not covering for you anymore, Bill. Don't you dare ask me to. I can't believe I've let you slide all this time. I let you put my family in danger!"

But then the anger in Maia's voice fell away, and she broke down and started crying.

"Oh no," she said. "This is all my fault."

The idea that Maia could blame herself for Elena's fate made Bill wince. "Please don't say that," Bill said. "It was me. I couldn't save her. There wasn't enough time. It just . . . happened."

But Maia didn't want to—or couldn't—listen. She took off running toward the Fountain, most definitely to go find an Elder.

As he watched her go, Bill let out a holler to clear his head. He had to focus on the next steps. He had to figure out a way to get Elena back.

But even if he could find a way to do that, Joe and his gang of humans had seen the Teddycats. How long would it take for them to discover Cloud Kingdom? What would they learn from Elena, and how?

Bill felt squished and helpless. A warm, dry wind blew across the Kingdom. He went to wipe his tears, but found that they had already been swept away.

A CROWD OF angry Teddycats gathered at the Fountain and formed a circle around Maia's family. Her mother, already frail, was stunned with panic and lingering disbelief. Her father was a coiled mess, pacing and darting with a barely contained fury.

Marisol and Big Bill were huddled with the Elders, nodding solemnly, while Bill was under strict orders to sit down and stay quiet. Everyone was staring at him, but nobody would meet his eye. The day still did not feel completely real. He really didn't want to cry again. Every few minutes a numbness crept into his mind, and he had to chase it away over and over again. He felt like he deserved the pain, like it was the least he could do.

Bill's biggest fear was that Elena was gone for good. His second was that the Elders wouldn't give him permission to help with the rescue mission. Rumors about what had happened, and what would happen because of it, were already whipping through the crowd, and with each one there were renewed calls for Bill's banishment.

Not that banishment meant much anymore if the humans were already on to them.

Bill tried not to be defensive. The truth was that he had knowingly pushed the boundaries of Cloud Kingdom. He had been a bad influence to younger, more impressionable Teddycats. He knew deep down that it was true he didn't mean for Elena to get hurt, but he had to admit that she wouldn't have been captured had it not been for him.

He needed to get Elena back. He would do anything to get Elena back. Of course, he couldn't say any of this aloud. He could only sit off to the side, on the edge of a mob, feeling very alone. A memory came to him, from a long time ago, when he had just been a little kitten. Bill had accidentally snapped a branch that swatted Maia right in her snout. While she ran around the Kingdom screaming, Bill zipped off into some deep brush behind his den and hid there the rest of the afternoon. Finally, his mother found him. She explained that Maia was fine, she was just scared and a little bit hurt, but now everything was back to normal. He apologized to Maia, who even apologized to him, and they shared a hug and a snack.

But during those hours he'd spent in the brush, thinking he was going to get kicked out for hurting a fellow Teddycat, he had tried to prepare himself for a whole new life.

Bill used to think that day in the brush was the absolute worst he could ever feel.

He wished he still believed that.

And just when he thought things couldn't get any worse, Omar approached. He wore a disappointed pout. Bill eyed him warily, but he was in no position to lash out. The space between them was clammy and clumsy with unspoken aggression.

"You really let us down today, Bill," Omar finally said, shaking his head. "You really let all of us down big-time."

"I'm sorry," said Bill, through gritted teeth.

"What are you going to do now? Where are you going to *live*?"

Bill stood up. They were snout-to-snout, and Omar didn't back down. He was definitely feeling more confident than he had the last time they spoke. And he definitely knew that Bill couldn't afford to look cruel or reckless right now. Bill glanced over at his parents, who were still whispering with the Elders. Big Bill had taught him to stand up for himself, but he'd also warned him never to fight. But what should he do in times like these, when it seemed the only way to stand up for himself was to fight? This was the kind of question that drove Bill batty. But today it didn't even matter. There was no way he could force Omar to see things another way, or even just shut him up.

"I'm not going anywhere," Bill said, finally.

"We'll see about that," Omar said through a pinched smile.

Chapter

 6

FINALLY, **THE ELDERS** spoke to the crowd. The scouts had been dispatched; their thoughts and prayers were with Elena and her family. The crowd dispersed, unsatisfied and still riled.

Back at the den, Bill sat glumly with his mother. Neither spoke for a long time. Outside they could hear Big Bill puttering around, applying fresh mud to the walls. This was the way he always worked through his anger. The angrier he was, the more dangerous the job he would take on. The last time Bill really messed up (he'd helped himself to someone else's garden), his father stayed on the roof of their den for almost two days, supposedly addressing a problem with the ventilation. Bill noticed that he always seemed to choose projects that were especially noisy. Bill would be curled up in his straw, feeling down, and the scrape and rip of his father's efforts would echo endlessly through the den. There was no escape, nothing to do but wait until he was ready to scold his son.

Bill started honing in on the very real, and very scary, possibility that his father might never speak to him again.

He glanced longingly out to the lane and was startled to see Felix strolling past in a slow, creaky prowl. The jaguar stopped just outside the den and, locking eyes with Bill, beckoned him outside to the lane.

Bill pointed at himself. "Me?" he said aloud.

His mother raised her head and considered him curiously, and Bill shut his mouth and resumed his sad, silent repose. When Marisol got tired of staring him down, she rose and began to assemble dinner, and Bill managed another look outside. Felix was still out on the lane, still staring right at him. Bill looked over at his mother, her shoulder thrusting with each punishing downstroke. Those roots were going to be well mashed. Confident that she wouldn't be able to hear him, Bill slipped out of the den and joined the jaguar down the lane.

"Tough day, Bill?" Felix said. His voice was deep, his eyes wide and penetrating.

"I guess I'm the worst Teddycat in the world," Bill said.

"Bad things happen to everyone," Felix said. "It doesn't mean they are deserved, or that it's always somebody's fault. Your parents, your friends, the Elders, they're scared right now. They have been away from the jungle for a long time, and they aren't ready to acknowledge just how easily this sort of thing can happen. They're in shock. All they can focus on is the pain."

"And what about you?" Bill asked. "You can see through the pain?"

Felix laughed gingerly. "I'm always in pain," he said, clutching his side. "You get used to it. The trick is to stop looking for someone to blame and start looking for solutions."

"All I want to do is get Elena back," Bill said. "That's the only way I can fix this, get Maia's forgiveness, and maybe save Cloud Kingdom from the humans."

"That's a tall order," Felix said, a hint of approval in his eyes. "What do you know about humans, Bill?"

"Humans?" said Bill. He rubbed his chin. "Let's see. Basic bipedal formation. Gangly appendages. Hair about the head . . . region."

"So, not too much," said Felix.

"Well, I know Joe, of course," Bill said. "Dressed in stolen snakeskins and furs, mouth full of gold."

"Well, I've had some run-ins with humans over the years," Felix said. "And I've found that, roughly, they can be divided into two camps. The first is a straight-ahead predator, here to wreak destruction for fun or profit. These types will burn down whole valleys just to smoke you out. They're here for the tusks and the hides and whatever else they can sell. You understand?"

"Sure," Bill said. "That's Joe."

"Right. Joe. Now, if Elena fell into one of his traps, well, I hate to say it, but she may be long gone by now. These Joe types don't tend to stick around after they've snagged something. They want to get it back to their den so another human—a different kind, one that never ventures into the jungle—can tell them if it's worth anything. But that doesn't mean Elena's lost forever. I've tracked my share of humans over the years, and the bad ones are especially sloppy about hiding their paths. So we could follow along and find their base. If we get there quickly enough, Elena might still be in her cage, a little frightened but no worse for wear."

Bill nodded. It sounded dangerous, almost thrilling, but more important, it sounded possible. "Wait," he said. "What are the other types of humans?"

"The others are a more . . . clinical sort," said Felix. "It's hard to explain. They don't have the smoke and razzle of the bad set. Rather, they are methodical, with better equipment, which makes them harder to track."

"I don't get it," Bill said. "What do they want?"

"My impression is that they want to study the jungle. Their intentions may be decent, but they are still powerful predators. And of course it's impossible to know for sure what these creatures want."

Felix smiled and shifted his weight. His joints made an audible creak.

"Listen, Bill. I love Cloud Kingdom. The Teddycats have been good to me. But you can't run away from the jungle. There will always be something hunting you. That's the way the world works. Sooner or later, the Teddycats will have to figure that out."

"Felix, do you know any Olingos?" Bill asked after a contemplative silence.

"Several."

"They're a good crew, the Olingos," Bill said. "You met my friend Luke. The two of us are building a fort. There's gonna be a swimming hole and everything. Well, there was gonna be one, before things got all messed up."

"The fort—is it another place to hide?"

Bill thought about it for a moment.

"I guess not," he said, finally. "When we first started work on it, maybe. But now I see it as a place to come together, if that makes sense."

"That makes perfect sense to me," Felix said. "And it's a goal worthy of much risk."

"Risk meaning . . . adventure?" Bill asked, lowering his voice.

"In my experience," Felix said, "the two often go hand in hand."

"So," Bill said, immeasurably grateful to Felix for giving him a reason to feel more hopeful. "We need to figure out which kind of humans took Elena and track them back to their den."

"Yes," said Felix. "And hopefully before they figure out what they've got."

Chapter

 7

BUT BACK IN the den, Bill realized that, despite the invigorating conversation with Felix, nothing had really changed.

The Elders wouldn't care what a jaguar had to say. He wasn't a Teddycat. In fact, he was in debt to them. And there was still the matter of Big Bill, who had yet to speak so much as a single word to his son since Elena's abduction.

Bill curled up in his straw, plugged his ears, and watched the pall he had created stretch and settle across the Kingdom. He wished he could go to Diego Bribon, a sinewy Teddycat scout with a wild mane, a pink scar where his left eye used to be, and an allergy to authority, for advice. The Elders tolerated Diego's salty disposition because he was an excellent scout and had most likely saved each of their lives at one time or another.

Diego lived in a dilapidated bachelor's den in the shady section of Cloud Kingdom. Sometimes, in the late afternoon, when he knew he could find Diego at home, whittling, Bill would pepper him with questions about the jungle. Diego was a warrior and, more than that, he was different from any other Teddycat Bill had ever known. Even Big Bill himself encouraged Bill's fascination with Diego. The respect was obvious in Big Bill's voice when he talked about Diego's bravery and service over the years, and Bill knew better than just about anyone how hard it was to win the respect of his father.

Unless it was an absolute emergency, it was best not to bother Diego before noon. But Bill knew he would be up and about today, having been sent out by the Elders to check the perimeter for signs of encroaching humans. He tried to shake off a descent into deeper doldrums by concentrating on a plan: He would wait until Diego returned, get his attention, and relay what Felix had told him. Surely there was no way such a seasoned scout would ignore valuable intelligence, even if it was from an outsider.

Suddenly, a commotion cut through the heavy quiet, and for a brief moment, Bill's heart flared with hope. *They'd found Elena!* But, no, it was just the rolling fireball of gossip accompanying the return of Diego and his partner, Jack, from their morning hitch.

Bill flew out of the den, and Marisol didn't try to stop him.

The Fountain area was filled with huddles of skittish Teddycats waiting for Diego to finish briefing the Elders. Bill spotted Maia but was too ashamed to even seek her eye.

Soon, a simple question started rippling through the crowd. *Where was Jack?*

The Teddycats were on the verge of panic. They began to cry out, demanding answers.

After what felt like far too long, Ramon, a hunchbacked Elder with a tangled gray beard, climbed the stone perch and signaled for silence. Diego stood beside him, steely and serious.

"In light of recent events," Ramon said, "we sent our scouts out early this morning to assess our security. The news they've brought back is not encouraging. A human attacked our scouts, capturing one. What's more, the attack exposed a scout's claw."

Diego's wiry frame slumped into a downcast expression, and Bill knew that Jack must have been the one captured.

"Our claws have long been symbols of our tenacity and perseverance," Ramon said. "They are a testament to our willingness and ability to fight for survival in a dangerous world. We protect our claws with strict rules because they are so valuable and, therefore, dangerous. Based on what we have recently witnessed, it's clear that our species, and our home and our way of life, is under attack. Therefore, the Elders have decided to place Cloud Kingdom on emergency lockdown, effective immediately. Please return to your dens and limit all noise and movement. We will share pertinent developments as they become available."

Ramon sighed.

"Be safe, and bless Cloud Kingdom."

MAIA WAILED. BILL rushed over to her side. She was crumpled over and weeping. This was bad. A lockdown meant no more scouts or rescue parties. It also meant that the Elders had decided that losing Elena and Jack was an acceptable price for their communal safety. But sitting around silently and waiting didn't seem like too sound a strategy to Bill, especially considering everything he'd learned from Felix. There was still so much about their situation they didn't know! What humans did Diego and Jack encounter? Were they the same humans that took Elena? And was it humans that had driven the Teddycats out of Horizon Cove?

But Bill had to put all that aside for the moment and focus on his friend.

Maia was still weeping, but the sobs were dry. She was wrung out, exhausted, and depleted. "So much for the rescue party," she said, resting her head on Bill's shoulder. "I had my mind all made up to head down there no matter what. Now, even if I found Elena, I won't be allowed back home! How does that make any sense at all? How can they *banish* me, just for risking my life to save another Teddycat? Explain that to me, Bill."

"I can't explain it," Bill said. "You're right. It makes no sense."

He wanted to tell her that they had the same plan; that in a perfect world, they would go find Elena together and find a new place to live; that Cloud Kingdom felt shriveled up, its glory sapped, its physical beauty at jagged odds with the dour dread and fear that had seeped in and overtaken the place. Instead, he just let her rest.

Chapter

 8

EVENTUALLY, **BILL WAS** forced to leave Maia's side. He was burrowed and therefore required back at home, where he chewed silently through a tense dinner with his parents, then dutifully retreated to his straw, where he curled up and drifted off into a fitful sleep.

The nightmares arrived, breathless and frantic. Bill felt himself falling through an endless canopy, into a field filled with traps and cages with sharp, rusted teeth. He saw a faceless horde vaulting over the Wall with terrifying ease. He saw Cloud Kingdom on fire, heard yelps of pain as Joe and other shadowy human-like figures advanced through the ashes, and then—

Bill woke with a start. He bolted upright, his claws bared and glinting. The moon was low in the sky, casting pale, insistent light across his straw. He imagined Maia awake across the Kingdom, too broken up to sleep. He imagined Elena and Jack behind bars, at the mercy of Joe. A thought pierced him: *What if he was the one out there all alone? What if he had fallen into that trap, and his friends and family weren't allowed to help?*

In the ghostly quiet Bill was hit with two undeniable truths: One, the lockdown was a tragic mistake, and two, he needed to do all he could to rescue the lost Teddycats. Consequences—doled out by the jungle, the humans, or the Elders—were beside the point.

Bill assembled a quick bindle with dinner scraps and a lucky nub of petrified wood, and tied it to his tail. As he crept toward the exit, he heard his father's snores reverberating through the den, filling it with a familiar feeling of warmth. He made a silent promise to return, then slipped out the door.

As he set out, Bill realized he'd never descended from Cloud Kingdom in the dark before. He took it slowly, surprised at his own patience. His mind was clear; all the fear and anxiety that pricked at his dreams had been snubbed out by a newfound sense of purpose and the crisp night air. Mist from the waterfall beaded on Bill's fur, which made crossing the Wind Tunnel all the more chilling. The usual scenic vistas were shrouded in darkness, leaving Bill one misstep away from the abyss. But he realized this had always been true, and pretending otherwise had led to many troubles.

Bill rode a lava chute the last third of the way down. The jungle floor was eerily still, nary a rustle or hoot. Usually the tree frogs would be making a racket. Was it a human invasion that had caused this cease in activity, or was it just a slow night? Either way, he was relieved when he finally reached Luke's den.

"*Psst!* Luke!"

He crouched and whispered his friend's name in increasingly husky tones, finally reaching a frustrated crescendo with a shrill whistle.

Luke's face, crusty and misshaped with sleep, emerged. He glanced around, blinking eyes adjusting to the darkness, passing right over Bill. "Huh?" he said.

"Down here!" Bill whispered.

"Bill?" Finally Luke's eyes fell on his friend. "What're you doing here?"

Bill bristled a bit at the question. He was still angry with Luke for interfering with his Elena rescue. But then Bill remembered what he was about to ask him to do.

"Shhh," Bill hissed, then softened his tone and the look in his eyes. "Secret-mission time, buddy. You up for it?"

"I'm game," said Luke, yawning.

He always was.

BILL WAS THINKING about the humans, trying to remember Felix's theory. It was hard enough to worry about Joe, but now he had to entertain the idea that there were more of them out there. It chilled him to imagine the jungle ripped apart by marauding humans. Cloud Kingdom, the forest floor, no place would be safe.

"I'm hungry," Luke said.

"It's the middle of the night!" Bill said.

"What, you never heard of a nocturnal snack?"

"Teddycats have a pretty disciplined feeding schedule," Bill said. "But by all means, dig up some grubs or whatever it is you like, if that's what it takes for us to get on with our mission."

"I'm not really in the mood for grubs," Luke murmured. "More like something sweet."

Bill sighed. "Well, if I've learned one thing recently, it's that the universe doesn't care about moods—yours, mine, or anybody else's."

"The universe is dumb," Luke said.

"It's definitely unfair," said Bill.

"Humans are allowed all sorts of moods, I'll bet," said Luke, chewing loudly on a root.

"That's the top of the food chain for you," Bill said. "Frees up a lot of mental space. Too bad they use it for storing evil plans and inventing new traps."

Luke stepped on Bill's heel. "Sorry," he said, his voice wet in Bill's ear.

They were making bad time. Bill's newfound patience, as refreshing as a cold lap of water earlier in the evening, was running thin. Also, he suddenly realized he had no idea where he was going.

"Where are we even going?" Luke said.

"I told you, it's a secret," Bill said, buying time.

Back in the den, with the moon interrogating him through the window and the weight of Cloud Kingdom on his shoulders, it had all seemed very clear. But now, down in the jungle, the wilderness was as untamed and unforgiving as ever. He weathered a tremble of uncertainty.

Just then, a dash of heat lightning silently lit up the sky and, for a brief moment, their surroundings. Luke's jaw was working hard on a root. Something sweet, indeed.

The flash of light jolted Bill with a dose of gumption.

He decided to start the search where his troubles began, just below the Crook.

THE CLEARING STILL bore marks of the struggle. He could see where the cage had rested: The grass was dented, with shallow scratching in the dirt. It hurt Bill to imagine Elena with her little claw bared, digging helplessly into the ground just before she was carried away.

Maybe Teddycats would be better off without their claws, thought Bill. As far as Bill knew, his species knew *how* to use them in every way—hunting, gathering, shelter, surgical procedures—except for the one they were allowed under only the most dire of circumstances: self-preservation. Maybe it was better to be unremarkable, squeak below the radar. Not that those circumstances helped the Olingos, who were continually forced to uproot and resettle at the whims of any invasive species that happened through their warren.

"Returning to the scene of the crime," said Luke. "Isn't that . . . dangerous?"

"It's the only lead we've got," said Bill. He circled the clearing until he found a trail marked by trampled underbrush. "This way," he said.

BILL'S UNDERSTANDING OF the jungle was limited to only a few landmarks—Cloud Kingdom access points, the fort, Luke's place—and the wide swaths of thick, unknowable wilderness between them. As they burrowed deeper he found himself growing increasingly disoriented, almost upside-down. The moon was slowly dropping. Soon morning would be upon them. Bill was fairly sure he could still turn tail and follow their own steps back to the clearing, but if they were forced to zig or zag or head for the trees and swing to safety (with Luke on his back, of course), they could potentially find themselves dropped down in the middle of nowhere.

Bill restored his resolve by remembering the way Maia's face had fallen when he told her the news about Elena. He shuddered. That tactic would work—maybe too well—for many years to come.

"I don't even know this Jack guy," said Luke. "Who's he again?"

"He's a scout," said Bill. "Remember I was telling you about Diego?"

"The old guy with one eye?"

"Right," said Bill. "Jack is his scouting partner."

"And he got taken by a human, just like that?"

"I'm not sure how it went down, exactly," said Bill. "But let me ask you a question: How long do you see yourself lasting against Joe? Smoke everywhere, shiny blade."

"Ha," said Luke. "That question's not fair, 'cuz, see, I'm not a big, tough Teddycat scout with a deadly claw just itchin' to pop out of my paw at the first sign of trouble."

Bill wheeled around. Now he and Luke were snout-to-snout in the misty moonlight.

"Do me a favor," said Bill. "Don't badmouth the Cloud Kingdom scouts around me."

"Hey, come on. You have to see things from an Olingo's perspective," said Luke. "Teddycat scouts have never helped *me* out any."

"Not everything is about you," said Bill.

"That's rich, coming from a Teddycat."

"What's that supposed to mean?"

"You sit around up there in your hidden Cloud fortress, passing judgment on all the animals struggling down here in the *real* jungle."

"That's not true," Bill said quietly.

"You think you've got problems, Bill? You want to talk about the food chain? We're at the mercy of more kinds of predators than you could imagine. Meanwhile, you guys have removed yourselves from the entire ecosystem. Good for you, but that makes you soft."

"Let me get this straight," said Bill. "*You're* callin' *me* soft?"

"That's right," said Luke. "Just because you have those claws and can climb faster than me doesn't mean you're stronger."

"Actually, that's *exactly* what it means," said Bill.

"All I'm saying is, I'm sorry about your friends, but in the grand scheme of the jungle, that's *nothing*."

Bill was fuming. He'd lost complete sight of why they were even down here together in the first place. The jungle was dark and foreign.

"I can't believe you," he said. "*You* are the whole reason I'm in this mess! Because of *you*, I can't hold my head up back home. Because of *you*, my friends are in danger. Because of *you*, the future of Cloud Kingdom is in jeopardy, and all because *you* were badgering *me* about a visit. Well, you got what you wanted. Happy now?"

"I don't know about *badgering*," said Luke. "That's a strong word."

"It is a strong word," said Bill, "but it's the right one."

"I was curious about Cloud Kingdom. You've always known that."

"Very curious," said Bill. "And you know what they say, Luke, curiosity kills the . . ."

Chapter

 **9**

LUKE TOOK A step, and suddenly something fastened around his leg and yanked him ten feet in the air. He dangled and thrashed in the darkness, whimpering and howling.

A trap.

Bill stood beneath him, dumbfounded. He didn't dare move.

"Bill, help!" cried Luke.

"Hold on!" said Bill, willing himself to action. After all, Luke had saved *him* from a human. Even if Bill begrudged him that decision, it had still demonstrated friendship and bravery, both of which he owed in return. He slowly scrutinized the ground in front of him to try to pinpoint the trunk of the tree hosting the trap. He found it and began to inch his way over.

Just as he was beginning to form a plan, Bill heard a rustle. He froze, looking all around. Then, a little ways off, he saw a shadowy shape stomping out of the darkness and into a ribbon of moonlight.

Joe.

As the shape drew closer, Bill had no doubt it was a human. It clutched a big branch in one paw and a shiny thing in the other, and then, with a clicking sound, the branch began to flicker and glow. All was still and brilliantly illuminated.

The human reached down and yanked a cord, and the net holding Luke lowered to the ground. Bill watched, paralyzed, as the human grabbed Luke by the scruff of his neck and swiftly deposited him into a cage in his other paw. Luke thrashed and screeched, bouncing against the steel grate.

The human's voice was an ugly growl.

Bill's fur went straight and prickly. It sounded the way he had always imagined Joe would. The human's light landed on Bill, and their eyes met.

The human cackled and made a lunge for Bill, but the cage, wiggly with Luke, banged hard against its leg, and the human yelped and staggered. Bill leapt into the underbrush, burrowed to the nearest stand of trees, and scurried up into the canopy. The human's angry glowing branch followed him, just a step behind. Bill could hear the human's heavy breathing as it waved the branch up and down, back and forth, jittery and determined.

Bill looked down. The human stood at the bottom of the tree, methodically scanning the lower branches. Bill sucked in his belly, made himself as small as possible, tucked his tail and his bindle under his rump, and squeezed his eyes shut. His claws were out, but hidden from the light.

The human bellowed in frustration.

Bill had been expecting a dangerous confrontation tonight—a daring jailbreak, to free Elena from the hapless Joe. But this was not at all what he'd had in mind.

The human's voice grew a touch softer, so Bill chanced a look. He peeked between his forearm and tail. The human's stilted warble, gray complexion, and yellow eyes matched the terrifying descriptions of Joe that young Teddycats used to share on nights when they'd camp out together in someone's leafy den. So too the huge boots and sagging jacket, the skin streaked with dirt and sweat, the bandana high on the skull, the hint of gold in a crooked, sadistic smile. The cage rattled as Luke shook with terror, his eyes searching for Bill. The flaming branch fell to the ground, and the human dropped a black sheet over Luke's cage.

Chapter

THE HUMAN STOMPED back into the darkness with a caged and braying Luke. As soon as Bill was sure he was gone, he blasted into full-blown panic mode. His mind raced as the world around him took on a threatening quality. Every branch and vine, every whistle and honk, every star in the sky and particle of mist announced fresh dangers.

Luke was right: Bill was soft. He was unprepared for daily battle with the most basic and even innocent elements of life in the jungle. He hadn't respected the ever-present dangers. He hadn't even noticed most of them. It was a ruthless place, always on the verge of violence, and now Luke's fate was the same as Elena's and Jack's. The jungle had spoken: Nobody was safe.

Bill could barely face the idea of bringing more bad news back to Cloud Kingdom. Maybe the Teddycats were better off without him. He should have let Joe take him, too. He should go right now and surrender to Joe. Better yet, he should let the Olingos surrender him to Joe, have them negotiate a swap for Luke. Once Joe got Bill, he could focus on freeing Elena and Jack. Never mind himself. He didn't deserve to return to Cloud Kingdom, let alone as a hero. Besides, if Felix was right, the humans weren't going to stop coming after the Teddycats and their claws. Bill remembered the human's creepy call and shuddered. No wonder the Elders preferred to hide up in the clouds. Who wanted to face a monster like that?

The human's sour smell was stuck in Bill's snout. He rubbed at it furiously. But wait—that stink was useful intelligence. Bill let his snout tingle with the lingering traces of his hunter.

With a sinking gut, he realized what a fool he had been to think he could do this—save Elena, declare Cloud Kingdom safe for all of the Teddycats—alone. It didn't even matter if his heart was in the right place. Going off alone was just another way to shirk his responsibility, a decision as narrow-minded as the Elders' rule forbidding anyone to leave Cloud Kingdom. If Cloud Kingdom was to be saved, they would have to do it together: all the Teddycats joining up, with one plan and one goal. Bill—with the best intentions—had chosen to sneak out at night, but the truly brave thing would have been to stay until morning and rally the Kingdom.

Bill knew he was going to need help—lots of it—but who was going to help him now? Luke was gone, lost to Joe. Maia was out of the question—he had already put her through too much, and besides, she had lost all trust in him. His parents would just punish him all over again for even giving voice to this idea. He needed guidance. He needed to seek out a bridge he hadn't burned yet, a heart he hadn't broken.

Suddenly, Bill slapped his head.

Of course! Who knew more about the jungle than Felix?

THE OLD CAT was up, puttering about the convalescence den. Bill wondered if he ever slept. Maybe the pain was too bad; maybe he missed his home too much. Maybe he was haunted by some terrible error in judgment. Was there *any* way to get through life at least somewhat unscathed, if it was possible to grow old and still have friends willing to talk with you and be seen with you?

Or maybe, Bill thought, Felix was just an early riser.

It was almost dawn, and the clouds were flushed pink with ascendant sun. But the beauty did little to soothe Bill. It only reminded him of all he had already risked, and all that might still be lost. Instead of returning, triumphant, with Elena and Jack, he was back with a heavier burden than ever.

Bill poked his head in further. Felix did not seem overly surprised to see him. "Good morning, Bill. How's the lockdown treating you?"

"Yeah . . ." said Bill. "About that."

"You don't strike me as an isolationist," Felix said. "Starting to chafe?"

"I've already violated the lockdown," Bill admitted. "I didn't even last a night."

"Hmm," said Felix. "Did you have a productive trip?"

"It was a total disaster."

"What happened?" Felix asked, his features creased with concern.

"I roped in a buddy to help me, and now he's been abducted," said Bill, rushing to get the words out. "Same as Elena, same as Jack."

"I see," Felix said. "Your friend the Olingo?"

"That's right, you've met him."

"I'm sorry to hear it."

"I shouldn't have dragged him into it," said Bill. "I just didn't know where else to turn."

"So where do you turn now?" Felix asked.

Felix was easy to talk to. Bill felt like he could speak more freely with him, abandon all the filters he tried to run his thoughts through when talking with other Teddycats. Of course, those filters never really helped. Bill was forever jamming his paw in his mouth, and then trying to kick up enough dust to cover his own tracks. But talking with Felix made him feel that he had greater access to his own thoughts, the way he used to feel with Maia before things got so complicated.

"Honestly?" Bill said. "I feel like I have only two options."

"Let's hear 'em," said Felix.

Bill cleared his throat. The smell of the human still burned in his snout. "Okay," he said. "Here goes. One: self-banishment."

"Ouch," Felix said. "And how does that sound to you?"

"It depends," Bill said. "Sometimes terrifying, sometimes great, like I could just retire to my fort or head out someplace completely new and different."

"But that's life as a Teddycat," Felix said. "You'll always attract attention. You're new and rare and extraordinary."

Bill followed the fantasy for a moment. "But what if I headed someplace quiet, and posed as a meerkat or something, and kept my claw hidden?"

Felix laughed. "Well, if that's your dream, I won't try to persuade you otherwise. But you do know that by doing that, you'd be following a long and frankly self-sabotaging Teddycat tradition, right?"

"And what's that?"

"Mistaking flight and hiding as anything other than a temporary solution. But never mind that for now. What's option number two?"

"Well, I actually don't even know," said Bill, overwhelmed all over again. "Another rescue mission, I guess."

"Go on," said Felix, one brow raised encouragingly.

"But a rescue mission would mean overturning the lockdown and challenging the Elders, and right now I don't have a whole lot of Cloud Kingdom support. I'm guessing most Teddycats would vote for option one."

"Meaning banishment."

"If things keep getting worse like this and I stick around, there's a good chance I could wake up in a stone-filled sack, sliding off the waterfall."

Felix considered this for a moment. "I don't think they'll wish you away, Bill, let alone help you pack your bags. You're an important and valuable member of Cloud Kingdom."

Bill scoffed.

"What? It's true," Felix said. "You have friends and persuasive ideas and charisma, not to mention respected parents. And try as they might to deny or ignore it, the Elders need you. Successful societies *need* rabble-rousers and troublemakers, my friend. Otherwise there'd be no progress or evolution. If old farts like me and the Elders ran the jungle, the whole place would shut down an hour before sunset so we could soak our joints and complain about the weather. Not to mention, I don't think you'd last five minutes posing as a plain old meerkat, Bill. No matter where you go."

"You're probably right," said Bill, feeling a bit dizzy.

"Always happy to hash it out with you, Bill," said Felix. He stretched and smiled as sunlight—the full brunt of which was still relatively new to him as a jungle-floor dweller—spilled through the cracks of his den. "But I'm not here to steer you either way. You're free to do whatever you think is right. In my experience, disasters like these sometimes make a creature feel like the world is shrinking, when actually it's finally opening up. What I'm saying is, you definitely have more than two options."

"Really?" Bill said. "Phew."

"That said, I will give you a little bit of advice, because that's what old guys like me do."

"I could use all of the advice I can get."

"The Elders have a meeting this morning. They're scared, and they're ready to run. But that's *their* problem. If I were you? I'd look back to the history between the Teddycats and the Olingos. Think about how their split has echoed through the jungle, through the years. The jungle doesn't have seasons, Bill. Therefore, life cycles can take years, even generations, to come back around. So, what can Teddycats learn from the life and death of Horizon Cove that might prevent the death of Cloud Kingdom?"

Bill sighed. His head was spinning. "I'll think about that. Really, I will, Felix. But first, I need to talk to Maia."

"Good luck," Felix said.

Chapter

BILL FOUND MAIA sunning herself atop her den, a front leg draped across her eyes. This was one of the places she went to be alone, and Bill approached cautiously. She didn't acknowledge his presence until he climbed up the side and scooted over close to her, and even then it was silent, cold.

The two of them sat there for a long moment while Bill worked up the courage and spittle to speak.

"Is this okay?" he finally asked. "Me being here?"

"Everyone's looking for you," Maia said, without glancing at him.

"I know," Bill said.

He pulled nervously on the mud and straw below them, a bad habit that was prevalent among the Teddycats. A gathering of anxious Teddycats could pluck a meadow clean in a half hour flat.

"You're basically a fugitive," Maia said.

"I'm not *trying* to hide, if that matters at all."

She considered him coolly. "Well, you seem nervous."

"I'm not trying to seem that way. And I'm not in hiding. You're not *harboring* me or anything. You won't get in trouble for talking to me."

"Ha," said Maia, mirthlessly. "First time for everything. So what're you so nervous about?"

Maia had this way of asking questions that landed like uppercuts. She could be very intimidating, which Bill had always admired about her (as long as it was unleashed on somebody else).

"Banishment, for starters," said Bill. "Armies of stampeding humans."

"I see," said Maia.

Bill sighed. "All right, here goes: I went down to the jungle in the middle of the night. To look for Elena. I talked Luke into helping me, and then he . . . well, he was nabbed by a human."

Maia's face fell again, and her head hung low against her chest. "Why does this keep happening?" she whispered. "What are we going to do?"

"Cloud Kingdom is changing, Maia. The jungle is closer than it's ever been before. I was talking to the jaguar . . ."

"Felix?"

"That's the one."

"He's a good egg," said Maia.

"Definitely," said Bill. "Felix thinks I should just keep trying with the Elders. In a respectful way, of course. To really make sure they see what they're giving up, and who they'll be leaving behind, if they just run away and keep hiding."

Maia seemed underwhelmed. "So that's the plan? You stroll up to the Elders and tell them to join you in a Bill Garra rescue operation? Despite a paw in every incident so far?"

"Look," said Bill, ears burning, "I know it sounds crazy. And like a long shot. But I see now why I've been failing so miserably at trying to help. It's because I've been trying to go it alone. I thought I'd be saving others the trouble, but I just wound up putting Luke—and everyone else—in danger. But this affects all of Cloud Kingdom, not just me and the animals I'm close to.

And if we're going to fix this, we've got to do it together."

"I'm sorry, Bill," Maia said, her eyes sad. "I just don't see what's so different this time."

"It's hard to explain," Bill said. He was frustrated. He wished he could show Maia how committed he was to saving Elena, but every time he tried things just got worse. "But I swear, it *is* different."

Maia just flicked her eyes up and down, taking in Bill's condition. "Think about it this way," he said. "I've got nothing left to lose."

With a jerk, Maia leapt up. She paced the sunny surface, veering closer to the edge with each lap. "That's your problem, Bill. You always think you've got nothing to lose. You probably would've said the same thing before Elena and Jack and Luke were taken. Yeah, things are bad. But they can get much, much worse. What about your parents? What would they say if they knew you thought you had nothing to lose? What about me, and the rest of my family? What about this whole place?"

"I *am* thinking about all that," said Bill, giving her a wide berth. "That's exactly . . ."

"Meanwhile, whatever's going to happen will happen, no matter what prank you pull or speech you make to the Elders. So grow up, and leave me alone."

Maia plopped back down again, looking exhausted now. Bill inched closer. Her pain was so obvious, it was like a fog.

"The Maia I know would be sharpening her claws, not sleeping in the sun."

"Well, this is the kind of shape *I'm* in right now."

Bill grasped his friend's shoulders. "Maia, please. I need you with me on this."

He could see the answer in her disappointed eyes, but he still held on to some old, deeply buried hope.

"I can't do it, Bill," Maia said. "I'm sorry. You're on your own."

Bill was silent for a long moment, chewing his lip until he regained composure. "Well, that's your right," he said. "Thanks for hearing me out."

"You're welcome," said Maia.

Bill gave her an awkward hug, which she accepted. It felt superficial, absent love or forgiveness.

"Hey, leave her alone!"

Bill wheeled around. There was Omar, down in front of the den, pointing and snarling.

"Just what I need right now," said Bill.

"Haven't you done enough, Garra? Why don't you let this family grieve in peace?"

"I was just leaving," said Bill.

"That's right, get lost," Omar said.

"Omar, take it easy," Maia said. "He said he's leaving."

"I'm sorry, Maia," said Omar, softening his tone. "I just can't stand to see you hurting like this, and then on top of everything else he's coming here and making everything worse."

Bill turned back to Maia and away from Omar, trying his best to shut him out. There was one more thing he needed to say, and he needed Maia to believe it.

"Maia, I will fix this," he said.

"Please, go," whispered Maia.

Bill nodded and slowly retreated down the den's back slope. He reached the ground and cut through the sweetmoss patch, and soon Maia was obscured by sunlight. But he could still hear Omar on the other side of the den, crowing triumphantly: "That's right, you'd better run!"

Chapter

THE ELDER MEETING was already under way.

Once again, Ramon stood before the Fountain and calmly outlined the disasters the Kingdom had already faced, as well as the additional disasters it might reasonably expect from the future. The gathered Teddycats were racked with panic: the exact opposite of the communal tizzy that overtook the population at rainbow-blessed sweetmoss harvests and other high holidays. Some particularly anxious Teddycats seemed on the verge of fainting.

Bill sliced his way through the crowd. If he stopped to reconsider his plan, even for a moment, he would lose his nerve. So he dropped his chin and kept pushing until he was kneeling before the Fountain. Ramon cast an eye downward at Bill but finished his thought. ". . . therefore, we must secure a new sanctum."

"Sir?" Bill said, jumping straight in, as usual. "May I address the Teddycats?"

Ramon smiled tightly at Bill. "Shoo, little Garra."

"There's something I need to say," said Bill.

Ramon's face was frozen for a moment, until he stepped aside with a dramatic flourish.

Bill couldn't believe it—Ramon was actually going to let him talk. But then, before he could even open his mouth to speak, he was walloped by a tidal wave of outrage. The crowd of Teddycats snarled and hissed, tried to shout him off the podium.

Then he spotted his parents, standing together near the back. Marisol offered a small smile. His father's features were stony, but Bill took some comfort in his steadfastness and predictability.

Finally, as the crowd began to tire, Bill watched a wave of exhaustion sweep through them. Bill had outlasted their anger, withstood the outburst, and yet he still wanted to stand before them and say his piece. He cleared his throat.

"Cloud Kingdom is my home," Bill began, and he was met with sleepy scowls. "I can't imagine life without this place. But it should not be a prison, or even some kind of exclusive hideaway. We are capable of so much more. There is real suffering on the jungle floor. And just because we're not down there to see all of it up close doesn't mean we can ignore our duties as citizens, as Teddycats, as jungle dwellers."

Bill stopped and took a breath, expecting to get hit with more anger. But, though there was definite tension in the crowd, they didn't fill the silence with hisses or shouts. They were listening.

"So let's stand up for ourselves," Bill said, seizing the chance to be heard. "Okay, so the humans know we exist. They've seen our claws, and soon they might figure out how to find our home. Right now, they're holding three of my friends—two Teddycats and an Olingo. I know that probably none of them would be missing right now if it weren't for me." Bill paused, feeling a ball of sad pressure build near his heart. He blinked once and kept going. "But I want to get them back, and I can't do it alone. I need help, from all of Cloud Kingdom. And if that means more exposure to humans and every-thing else down there . . . well, I think that's the risk we have to take. Because a sanctuary is not a sanctuary if it protects only animals strong enough to leave when the going gets tough. If we do nothing to help Elena, Jack, and Luke, then we're no better than the humans, or any other predator. Look how lucky we are! We can do so much good and help so many down in the jungle. Why not be proud of that and step forward?"

The gulf between Bill and the crowd had slimmed and somewhat softened. That rippling static of discontent remained, but with less braying, fewer bared teeth.

"So. Is anybody with me?"

Nobody made a sound. Were they all choked up and unable to speak? Bill himself was trembling with adrenaline, and he couldn't see straight. His only plan had been to speak from the heart and hope for the best. He didn't realize until now how strong his convictions really were, and that they had just been waiting for him to find the courage to share them. He glanced at his parents, but they wore only blank smiles.

"What do you say?" Bill said, ready to bring it home. "Let's do—"

"Get out of here, Garra!" shouted a Teddycat somewhere in the middle of the crowd.

"This is all your fault, you little jerk!"

"Boo!"

Bill threw up his arms in defense. "Wait!" he said. "Hold on, there's more! We can—"

"Boooooooooo!"

Bill surrendered. He stood up there, his chin on his chest, feeling foolish and lost. Finally Ramon nudged him off to the side with a subtle smirk, then got to work restoring order and calm among the Teddycats. As the crowd began to disperse, still murmuring insults under their breath, Bill trudged down from the Fountain, resigned to a life of exile.

Chapter

 13

BILL AND HIS mother took the long way back to their den, looping around the Kingdom. Big Bill Garra had decided to stay at the Fountain to debrief Ramon and discuss defense policies with the Elders. Bill knew exactly what would happen: The Elders would show him the courtesy of listening to him, but they weren't going to change their minds just because Bill was his son.

"I guess you and Dad are probably pretty much fed up with me," said Bill.

Marisol rubbed his head. "We know you're a good kitten, Bill. We're just worried about you."

"I wish I could stay here with you guys and just hope for the best. But I can't. I'm responsible for what happened to Elena, Jack, and Luke. You get that, right?"

"I get it," said Marisol.

"Good."

He turned away from his mother and yawned. Fatigue pinched his bones. His eyes itched. He couldn't remember the last time he had slept through the night. Grimacing, he swallowed the sleepy taste from his mouth, rubbed his eyes with his paws, and took three sharp breaths.

"You're tired," Marisol said. "I can tell."

"No way, I'm fine," Bill said. "Just got another wind."

"Don't try to hide from me, buddy," Marisol said. "I'm your mother."

"I'm aware of that, Mom."

"You're a brave little Teddycat, you know that? A little fresh sometimes, but brave."

"That doesn't seem like the popular opinion right now."

"I'm serious," Marisol said. "Forget all that. I'm going to tell you something, Bill, but you can't repeat it to anyone, no matter what. Okay?"

"Okay," Bill said, his little ears perking up.

"I'm serious," said Marisol. "You have to promise. If you tell anybody, I'll deny it."

"All right, I promise!"

His mother had never struck Bill as a particularly mysterious soul. Her priorities were unwavering and well-known. She lived for her family and her community, and she believed in kindness and selflessness. In other words, she was predictable, just like Bill's dad. Bill almost always knew where Marisol stood and where she could be found. She was supportive of Bill Sr.'s political ambitions, though she was far more passionate about misting the garden or delivering baskets of sweetmoss to neighbors in need, or caring for injured visiting creatures with her famous healing balm mixtures. So Bill had a hard time believing his mother was harboring a secret so big she'd forbid her son from acknowledging it in public.

"Then here goes," Marisol said, looking both up and down and behind her. They were standing on the outer rings of the Kingdom, the sheer face of the volcano rising before them. Seeing nobody, Marisol grabbed Bill by the arm and leaned into him. "I agree with you."

"Wait," began Bill, head swimming. "How so, exactly?" he asked.

"Remember our last talk?" said Marisol. "About the dangers of interacting with the jungle?"

"Sure," said Bill. "You scared me pretty good."

"Well, I wanted to tell you then, but it didn't seem like the right time. But that was before Elena and Jack went missing. I didn't realize how close we were coming to being exposed. And I certainly had no idea how much you were ready to sacrifice. But I agree with you. I don't believe Teddycats will ever reach their potential if we keep our heads in the clouds. And I don't think the Kingdom should be a secret. I think we need to exchange information, combine resources, join the party."

"Yes, that's exactly what I'm talking about!" said Bill. "But wait, why didn't you say anything back there, when everyone was booing me?"

"There are all sorts of grown-up reasons why I couldn't speak up back there. And if you decide to go down to the jungle, I won't be able to go with you. I'm not proud of some of the reasons keeping me quiet. It's complicated, but I just need to get this off my chest before you leave: I believe in what you're doing, and I believe in you. Maybe someday we will all return to Horizon Cove together."

"Wow," Bill said. He could barely think of what to say. "Thanks, Mom."

Marisol rubbed Bill's head again and wiped a tear from her eye.

"Now give me a hug," she said. Bill burrowed his snout into his mother's chest. It was warm and comforting, just as it had been a million times before.

"You are just the most perfect, wackiest possible combo of me and your father."

"Isn't that what usually happens with kittens?" Bill said.

"I guess so," Marisol said with a laugh.

They separated. "Remember: Keep my little confession under wraps."

"I *said* I promise," said Bill. "Believe in me? Believe in that."

"I do," said Marisol. "Now. How can I help? What do you need for your trip? If I were you I'd bring plenty of sweetmoss to barter. At the very least it might soften somebody up."

"That's a good idea," said Bill.

"And speaking of that," said Marisol, "I know there's not a lot of time to rest, but when was the last time you had a proper meal?"

"I could eat," said Bill, rubbing his belly.

They resumed down the lane and arrived at the Garra den, only to find Felix and Diego waiting for them. For the first time, Bill was confronted with the full extent of Felix's dignified bearing, his broad shoulders and proud jaw, all that remained of a slinky prowling gait despite his advanced age.

"Good afternoon, Mrs. Garra," said Felix.

"Good to see you up and about, Felix," said Marisol. She smiled and nudged Bill forward, then excused herself and went into the den.

"That was quite a speech, Bill," Felix said.

"Yeah," Diego said to Felix, ignoring Bill, "think he really believed any of it?"

"I do, every word!" Bill said defiantly.

Normally Bill would never have challenged Diego like that, but from the scout's sly tone, he suspected it was what he wanted. Bill tried hard not to stare at Diego's scar, but then again that was one of only two options. All that was left of Diego's missing eye was the jagged line where his fur would not grow. The rest was filled in with legend. There were conflicting accounts, about different battles against different foes.

"I believe in you, Bill Garra," said Felix, giving Bill an excuse to break his gaze. "Which is why I'm going to accompany you to the jungle."

The moment took on a shimmery, dreamlike quality. Felix's validation and partnership had taken

Bill from the depths of despair to the heights of hope and pride. He struggled to regain his wits, and could respond only with a wild fist pump that spun him around.

"Aye," Diego said. "And I'll come along as well. I owe it to my mate, Jack."

"Okay!" said Bill, excited. "I believe we officially have a posse."

"Hey, me three!"

Bill turned around, confused, and Felix and Diego followed his lead. There was Omar, with his arms crossed in a bold stance, in the middle of the lane.

"Now who's this li'l bugger?" said Diego, already gone cranky again.

"Oh, brother," said Bill, then took Omar aside. "Hey, Omar, quick question: Are you insane?"

Omar rubbed the back of his neck. "Look, I know we have our differences . . ."

"That's one way to put it," said Bill. "Didn't you just run me out of my best friend's yard?"

"She used to be my best friend, too!" said Omar.

It had been a long time since either one of them had acknowledged the distance that had grown between them. Bill wondered how much would remain if they blew off the dust. It had been mostly a question of awkwardness more than personality, the natural chafing between three competitive personalities.

"Look, I'm not saying we'll ever get back to me, you, and Maia, the way we used to be," Omar said quietly, "but Maia is still my friend. I want to help bring Elena home."

"What if, after all this, 'home' is some place different than Cloud Kingdom?"

"Wherever home might be," said Omar. "Wherever we're together."

"That's mighty decent of you, Omar," said Bill. "Is that the only reason?"

Omar laughed. "I guess . . . Well, it's stupid, but I've always wanted a shot at being a hero, you know? At first I was happy to watch you get creamed by the crowd at the Fountain, but then I realized . . . what he's proposing, it's pretty darn heroic."

"So this whole time I thought you hated me," Bill said, "but really you were just totally jealous. It's all starting to make sense now."

"Okay," Omar said, "I wouldn't say *jealous*. Let's maybe slow it down a little bit."

"If you say so, buddy," said Bill. "So, should we shake on it?"

"Sure," said Omar, sticking out a paw.

Bill did the same, but then hastily retracted it. "Wait," he said, eying Omar suspiciously. "Is this a prank?"

"No."

Bill narrowed his eyes. "Are you a spy?"

"No!"

"Well . . . okay, then," Bill said, then stuck his paw out again. They shook on it, and Bill introduced him to the old jaguar.

"Welcome aboard, Omar," Felix said. "I've met your father. He's a very enlightened Teddycat."

"Thank you," said Omar, blushing a bit.

"All right, enough of this dilly-dally," said Diego, roughly mussing the fur of Omar's head. "Now what?"

"Best to leave as soon as possible," said Felix, with one eye on the shifting afternoon light. "So go home and get your gear, Omar, but pack smart. We'll meet back here at dusk."

Chapter

BILL WAS JITTERY with nerves when Felix, Diego, and Omar came to collect him. They each had bindles tied to their tails. Diego wore a serious expression, his brow shading his scarred eye. Felix was doing his best to hide his limp, but it remained noticeable despite his stoic stance. Meanwhile, Omar stayed mum, making Bill think he was still adjusting to his newfound bravery and all the attendant consequences. His bindle seemed heavier than the others. Knowing his fussy mom, Bill figured she'd probably panicked and overpacked it with bulky bedding straw and other unnecessary gear.

"Go easy on the treats," said Felix when he saw the dinner scraps all over Bill's face. "We need you to stay nimble."

"I just fixed him something light," said Marisol, exiting the den and setting a basket down in front of them. "And here, I put together a little something for the group."

"Much obliged, Mrs. Garra," Diego said, in a voice softer than his usual growl.

"It's just some water, berries, figs, and sweetmoss," said Marisol. "I told Bill I thought the moss might be useful down in the jungle."

"Excellent thinking," said Felix. He cracked the basket and admired the goodies within. "Though I'd better sample a bit just to be sure."

"And I'll provide that *crucial* second opinion," said Diego.

"Please, help yourself," said Marisol. "You too, Omar."

But Omar looked too nervous to eat. His cheeks ballooned at the offer, as if he were chewing on air and barely keeping it down.

"Easy, Mom," Bill cautioned. He knew from experience that sometimes his mother had a tendency to push food on people no matter how green about the gills they appeared. It was obvious to him that, on some level, she truly believed that there was nothing she couldn't fix with some fresh, hot grub. And Bill and his father were usually willing to test that theory.

"Well," said Marisol, "whenever you're ready."

Though she smiled, it was clear from her bittersweet tone that the impending departure and uncertain future of her only child and his motley crew were finally coming to home to her. Still, it seemed everyone in the den had an unspoken agreement to ignore it. At least until they finished chewing.

There was a scratching at the entrance to the den. Omar was the most obviously startled by the noise, but Felix and Diego were on edge enough to whip their heads around. Diego even hastened into a defensive fighting stance, though he relaxed (somewhat) when he saw that it was only Big Bill Garra, wearing a customarily long face.

He established himself squarely in the center of the den and acknowledged the group with a curt nod. In many ways, Big Bill was the ideal carrier of bad news. The quietly stern way he delivered emotional gut punches often made the victim feel like they were getting off easy. For starters, he looked the part. His upper lip had a natural, rippled hitch, which left one of his more fang-like incisors permanently exposed and gave him a grim, determined expression. His ears were permanently perked, his brows thoughtfully uneven above cold eyes (Bill had inherited his father's unwavering stare). Big Bill appreciated thorns over flowers, or at the very least saw them as equally valuable. He was fierce, difficult, largely humorless, and distracted by danger and other pressing concerns. He valued quiet—not for the peace it brought but for the vigilance it implied.

"The Elders have come to a conclusion," he began. His voice was hoarse as ever, as if it had been shredded long ago while screaming for help and never recovered.

Bill was ready to listen to whatever his father needed to say but was certainly happy to have Felix and Diego in the room with him. They were fighters—surely his father could see that. Surely he could understand their motivations and respect their choice to venture into the jungle. *As if they even had a choice!* Bill wanted to say, but he knew better than to interrupt his father.

"If you choose to leave on this mission, you will not be able to re-enter the Kingdom. We are sealing up all entrances. The Wall will be patrolled with guards, who will attack trespassers on sight."

Marisol emitted a tiny yelp. Bill wanted to comfort her but remained where he was.

"The Elders have weighed the risks," Big Bill continued. "If you return, with or without those we've already lost, they feel there's a good chance you will expose our community."

Bill and Omar exchanged glances, but Felix and Diego were all business as they kept their steadfast gazes forward.

"I don't say this to scare you, or in hopes of changing your mind," Big Bill said. "You have good reason to leave, just as we have good reason to stay. I share the Elders' decree not necessarily because it reflects my views or because I don't support your goals, but because it is valuable information."

Bill felt dizzy, sideswiped. The world had taken on a shimmery, impermanent quality.

"Good luck," said his father, the words heavy with finality.

"Thank you, Mr. Garra," Felix said. "Sincerely."

"Yessir, thanks for lookin' out," Diego said.

Big Bill offered only another, deeper nod.

Bill went to his mother, leaning against her for support. She clutched him with uncertainty. He could feel her heart beating, fast and afraid, through her chest and into his own.

Felix lifted his injured leg with two paws and placed it gingerly on the den floor.

"As you are all well aware, I am neither a Teddycat nor a Cloud Kingdom native," Felix said, "so I will leave my three comrades to decide the fate of this endeavor."

He stuck his head out of the den. Sunlight pierced through the clouds and illuminated the sheen of his coat. He closed his eyes and basked in the warmth. "This sure is a beautiful place," he said. "Please know that I will be content with whatever you choose. Thank you for the meal. Good day."

He stepped out, and there was a long silence in the wake of Felix's departure.

"This don't change nothin'," grunted Diego.

"I'm happy to hear that," said Bill, though suddenly everything sounded like it was underwater. Looking around the den, he passed quickly over Omar's fallen face, which reflected the terror and dread he himself felt. But he really was happy to hear that Diego still wanted to go. One reason he wanted comrades in the first place was to ensure action, to spur him along when the going got tough and the stakes were raised. Well, the stakes were about as high as they could get. So if Diego was still game, Bill wasn't about to back out.

"Omar, nobody will judge if you want to stay here," Bill said. "We appreciate your support no matter what."

Omar gulped, then mustered all the resolve he could manage into his face. "No. Let's go save the day."

Chapter

BILL'S CREW ASSEMBLED on the Wall for one last farewell.

In the back of his mind, Bill remained hopeful that Maia might come to see him off, but now, with everything finally, irrevocably on the line, he knew whatever words he might blurt would be hollow and worthless. He would either save Elena and, in doing so, change the course of Teddycat civilization, or else he would languish in banishment or meet some other, even more grisly end.

Maia didn't need to know that he was doing this for her. What if things went wrong? She didn't need that guilt gnawing away at her in the middle of the night, the mystery of their final, doomed descent into the jungle casting a shadow across the rest of her life.

Bill's new philosophy, born of Maia's disappointment: If you do something for somebody, do it quietly or not at all. Oh, and honesty above all else. Maybe if he'd adopted these mantras a while back, things might have worked out differently. Still, if he was being *truly* honest, he had to admit he would have felt much better if Maia had shown up at the Wall so he could see her face at least one more time before he left home.

The Wall straddled two worlds, the quilted pink of Cloud Kingdom in the midst of its peaceful gloaming, and the frenzied jungle, barely imaginable through heavy humidity and a thick fog the color of yolk. They could hear the distant howls of the Wind Tunnel and the crush of the waterfall. Bill's neck tingled as a cool Kingdom breeze brushed his fur, perhaps for the final time.

Saying goodbye to his parents had not been easy. His father wished him luck, again. His mother's heart continued its crazed patter. Bill had felt swollen and stilted with emotion, afraid that if he let those feelings loose he might lose all his nerve or even melt completely. The occasion was so fraught and momentous it was almost awkward, like trading heartfelt farewells with a friend, only to see them again later that day. It felt too long and too quick at the same time.

"Drink it in, lads," said Felix, as the setting sun crept down the face of the volcano and filled the Kingdom like a bowl.

Bill almost didn't turn around—he was afraid it would be too much to bear—but when even Diego couldn't contain a mournful grunt of emotion, he turned on his heel and let the full majesty of the Kingdom smack him right in the face. It was beautiful.

"DON'T RUSH AHEAD, Bill," said Felix. "Let's stay together."

"I wouldn't call it rushing," mumbled Bill, as they slowly descended to the tree line. But if he didn't mind each step, he leapt well ahead of the others. Felix's injury slowed their progress to a maddening plod, and even Diego, the weathered scout, was a bit stiffer than Bill would have imagined. But it was Diego who brought up the rear, slowly, his good eye narrowed, a tight bundle of vigilance. Meanwhile, Omar had essentially been designated Felix's valet, keeping a steady leg at the ready should the old cat stumble on loose rock or get struck by a sudden bout of vertigo.

Though at times frustrating for Bill, their trip down to the jungle did remind him of the dangers of that journey and the natural defenses of Cloud Kingdom. Felix had almost been blown away in the Wind Tunnel—his fur rippling loose like a cape as he bore down against the gales—and the molten rock was smooth and fast.

Bill was itching to rip through the canopy, vine by vine, until his eyes watered from the speed. But even after the ground grew crunchy and stable with vegetation, they still moved slowly, deliberately, paying painstaking attention to their surroundings.

Soon after they left, Bill noticed that Felix and Diego used a system of paw signals to communicate silently. Bill wasn't sure if this was a secret jungle language he was supposed to know (he *did* skip a lot of lessons to hang out in the jungle with Luke) or if Felix and Diego were just signaling to each other to talk about, or above, him, the way his parents used to spell things out (D-E-S-S-E-R-T, B-E-D-T-I-M-E) before he wised up and cracked that code.

"Where are we even headed, anyways?" Bill asked while the crew took a breather beneath an umbrella tree.

Felix had his eyes closed. Diego lapped some water loudly. Omar looked homesick.

"The Olingo den," said Felix, eyes still shut. "We

need to assemble a coalition, and that starts with making peace with the Olingos."

"Good luck, mate," Diego scoffed. "You know those lazy 'lingos, always want something for nothing."

There were a few things Bill wanted to say to that, but he figured it was too early in the mission for a confrontation. Still, Luke's honor, and life, was at stake.

"That's exactly the type of thinking we need to move beyond," Felix said, eyes open now.

Empowered by Felix, Bill reconsidered. "My friend Luke is an Olingo. And I can tell you, he is a friend of the Teddycats."

"We all know about your friend Luke," Omar said bitterly. "Remember, you snuck him into Cloud Kingdom and pretty much unleashed chaos?"

"That the one got yanked up in a tree-trap?" Diego asked.

"That's the one," Bill said, glaring at Omar.

"Tell me about that trap," Diego said.

"What do you want to know?" Bill asked.

"Where was it? What set it off? How fast did Joe respond?"

"Oh," Bill said. He squinted and tried to focus. Fatigue made everything murky, and the film of fear, mixed with that night's spooky moonlight, played tricks on his memory. "Right. Well, it all happened very quickly. One second we were on the ground, on a trail near where Elena was nabbed, and the next Luke was in the air, upside-down."

"And the human?" Diego asked impatiently.

"Oh, Joe came right away," Bill said. "The light followed me everywhere. I barely had time to rip on out of there."

"Too bad you couldn't have followed him," Diego said. "Then we might have a real place to start instead of being on this wild toucan chase."

"We have a starting point," Felix said. He rose and propped himself against the tree. "That's better than nothing. We're two klicks from the Olingo den. Now, what's done is done. Is this the perfect team? The perfect situation? Of course not. But tell me, Diego, when was the last time anything was ever perfect in the jungle?"

"Well, things have been a little *too* perfect, maybe," Diego said.

"And how did that work out for you?"

"Lookin' back, I might say it got me so I wasn't as sharp as I should've been," Diego admitted. "A bit lackadaisical."

"Exactly," said Felix. "Nobody's perfect, so that's not what I'm asking for. What I *am* asking for is this:

Stick together and have the next fella's back. No more sniping, no more fantasies. If we walk like a team and talk like a team, our chance at success will rise from nil to slim. Can we agree on that?"

The crew mumbled and turned wayward eyes to the sky, examined their paws.

"I said, can we agree on that?"

"Yes," Omar said, too loudly.

"Sure," Bill said.

"Suppose so," said Diego.

"Good."

Chapter

EVEN DURING UNCERTAIN times like these, it was hard for Bill to resist the excitement of the jungle. He anxiously led the way as they approached the Olingo den. Familiar landmarks warmed his heart until he remembered the purpose of his visit. On the plus side, Felix's limp seemed to be improving. Whether that was due to the heat in the jungle or the stretch of exertion, Bill had no idea.

Bill was supposed to stay with the group, but he wanted to make sure the Olingos saw him first. They knew him. He didn't want them taken by surprise, alarmed by the sight of a jaguar and a one-eyed Teddy-cat at their door, asking for help.

The Olingo den was always quiet and a bit messy, kind of like what Bill imagined a king vulture nest to look like. The den consisted of a stand of shabby trees, awkwardly gnawed into a beehive of warrens and tunnels. Higher up in the tree crowns the Olingos stored their scant supplies and few valuables. It's possible this tendency toward disorganization was connected both to the Olingos' historical sense of impending doom *and* the nasty stereotypes spouted by Teddycats. But Bill could see that the Olingos understood their position on the jungle food chain better than almost anybody, Teddycats included, and if the Teddycats didn't see their reflection in the fate of the Olingos, well, they weren't looking hard enough.

The Olingos were very industrious, especially given their relative physical weakness—and lack of powerful claws. This is what Bill had wanted to say back at the powwow, if he hadn't been too nervous to cause a stir. Just because they didn't have a stately refuge like Cloud Kingdom to call home didn't mean they wouldn't know what to do with one, or that they wouldn't keep it tidy and humming and happy with ritual and community.

Out of habit, Bill led the group right up to Luke's usual nest, only to experience a near-heart attack when Luke himself popped out of the scrub.

"Hi, Bill!"

Bill skidded to a stop. His brain felt slanted. Was he seeing things? He hadn't slept for days, the stress was real enough to taste metallic in his mouth, and the circumstances were bizarre enough to play tricks on anyone.

"Luke?" he whispered, wide-eyed. "Is that you?"

"That's right, I'm back, baby!" Luke did a little spin and flip.

He seemed to be in good spirits and physically intact.

"For a minute there I thought I'd lost my mind," Bill said. "What happened to you? Tell me everything!"

"Wait a minute," said Luke, peering down the path behind Bill. "Who's that with you?"

"That's our group," Bill said. "From Cloud Kingdom. We came to find you. Well, we came to tell the Olingos that we were *committed* to finding you. And Elena and Jack. But wait, how did you escape the humans? When I left they had you wrapped up like root mash in a palm leaf."

"Yeah, thanks for that, by the way," said Luke.

Just as Bill was about to reply, Felix, Omar, and Diego approached.

"Who's this?" Diego said.

"It's Luke!" Felix said.

"Hello, Luke," Omar said coolly. "I thought you were with the humans."

"I was!" Luke said.

They stood there in the jungle's humid static for a moment, Luke just grinning until even Felix began to tap his paw impatiently.

"So spit it out, already!" Bill said.

"Look, I'll tell you everything. But can you at least come inside the den first? This isn't Cloud Kingdom; you can't be so loud."

Luke looked around, clearly thinking about predators, and Bill and Felix took the hint.

"He's right," said Felix. "Let's go on inside."

It took a little while, but eventually everyone's frayed nerves were soothed, diplomatic relations were repaired, and the Selva family welcomed the visitors into their section of the den. Between the trees, there was a leafy, shaded patch where the air was cooler and the ground was soft. Diego and Felix both slumped down with a sigh, while Bill and Omar looked on with jealousy as Luke and his family stuffed their faces with the sweetmoss and figs.

"So the humans . . ." Bill prompted, after the Olingos had finished chewing and thoroughly licking their paws.

"Right, the humans," Luke said. A belch ripped out of his mouth, impressively loud considering how tiny his gut was. "So," he said, addressing the entire group, "I was out with Bill, helping him look for Elena, when, next thing I know, I'm dangling from a tree!"

Luke's mother, Doris, was a pudgy but powerfully built Olingo. She shook her paw and squealed at the very mention of the human's trap.

"After the human gave up looking for Bill, it cut me down and carried me to its den. It was a real nasty place."

Now Bill's ears were perked. "Do you remember how to get there?" he asked.

"Bill," Felix scolded, "let him speak."

"Sure," Luke said to Bill, after offering Felix a little smile. "It's not too far. But . . . I don't know if you'd want to go. Like I said, it's nasty. Dark and loud, with a fire and lots of smoke. Oh, I saw another Teddycat—"

"You did?" Omar interrupted, speaking for the first time since being inside the Olingo den.

"I did. But it wasn't Elena . . ." Luke said, and Omar's face fell.

"Must've been Jack, then," Diego said.

"How . . . how is he?" Bill ventured.

Luke looked away. When he turned back, his eyes were welled up with tears. "I'm sorry. I couldn't really see much. But . . ." He stopped, then looked toward Doris, who gave him a quiet nod of encouragement. "It sounded like they were hurting him."

Diego was silent. Felix placed a paw on his shoulder.

"What about Elena?" Bill asked quietly.

"I didn't see any sign of her," Luke said. "I wasn't there long. I saw the smoke, the fire. I heard the humans shouting. I heard . . . Jack. And then, suddenly, I was free."

"Free!" hollered Freddy, Luke's father.

"Wait, slow down," said Diego. "Slow down. You escaped?"

"Sorry, I got a little ahead of myself. When I first got there, the human threw me into another cage. All of a sudden, a super-bright light was shining right in my eyes, practically blinded me! I balled up in the corner, but even though I couldn't see anything I guess the humans could still see me, because then the human started prodding me pretty good. I only saw its face for a second, when the light went away. Its head was huge, with dark eyes and a strong smell."

"Was it Joe?" Omar asked.

Bill knew it wasn't the time to tell Omar that the Olingos had a different relationship with the humans, that they didn't separate Joe from the others they saw every day below the canopy.

"There's no way he'd know for sure," said Diego.

"Then what happened, Luke?" Felix asked, and Bill was grateful that he was the one to change the subject.

"Then, after the blinding and the poking, I must have done something to make the human angry, because all of a sudden its face turned red and . . . boy, I thought that was it. I mean, I thought I was a goner. The human reached for me with a grubby paw, and I closed my eyes real hard, wishing I was anywhere but there, but then . . . nothing happened. I heard a big bang overhead, and the cage rattled—like what happens when the earth quakes—and so I opened my eyes, and the cage was open. I took the chance and I ran!"

"That's it?" asked Bill, incredulous.

"That's it. Nothing chased me or anything. In fact, I swore I saw it just sitting there, by that mean, smoky fire, watching me as I scampered off."

Nobody said a word.

"I'm sorry about your friends," Luke said. "I don't think there was anything I could have done to help them. Like I said, I didn't see Elena, and Jack . . . well, I think I was too late."

"It sounds like you did all you could, Luke," Felix said quietly. "Thank you."

Luke looked up at Felix gratefully again.

"That human was probably looking for your claws," Felix said. "I'll bet that when it saw you didn't have any that look like your friend's here, he let you go."

Of course, thought Bill with a sinking heart. The human thought they'd captured something new. A Teddycat. "You said the human prodded you?" Bill said.

"Yeah," Luke said.

"Where? Your paws?"

"All over," said Luke. "But yeah, definitely my paw."

"I can't stand to think of those no-good crooks messin' with Jack," said Diego, his gravelly voice sounding somewhat soggy.

"He will be remembered as a great and brave Teddycat," said Felix.

"What good's all that?" Diego scoffed. "The Elders left him to die."

"That's why we're here," said Bill. "That's why we're asking the Olingos for help."

Doris and Freddy groaned, breaking up the solemnity that had settled over Bill's group. Bill looked at their threadbare fur, streaked with a dull gray, dulled by exhaustion and perpetual terror.

"So now the Teddycats *need* the Olingos," Doris said. "That's rich."

Freddy laughed mirthlessly. His dour features were framed by a thin, puffy mane. "Funny how you only come down here when you *need* something."

Bill instinctively opened his mouth to respond, but then, remembering his follies over the last few days, shut it. He looked to Felix, who nodded encouragingly.

"You're right," Bill ventured. "About why we're here. We do need your help. And if we don't at least *try* to squash our differences, then we're all in trouble."

"Oh, please. You see it yourselves," Freddy said. "They don't want us. They want you. They want your precious *claws*."

"Ironic, isn't it?" said Doris.

"In case it's news to you, 'lingos," Diego snarled, "the way to Cloud Kingdom goes right through your dirty little den."

Doris and Freddy exchanged defiant glances. "Tell you what," said Freddy, his spine straightening with a crackle. "We'll bring this to our Elders, and they'll take everything said here into consideration. But I'll tell you one thing. It will take a real disaster to bring the Olingos and the Teddycats together again."

"That disaster is exactly what we're trying to avoid," said Felix.

Doris scratched behind one of her droopy ears.

"Does your little search party represent all of Cloud Kingdom?"

What should they tell them? Too much truth might scare off the Olingos, but they didn't want to mislead them. The Teddycats looked to Felix, who nodded again at Bill.

"You'll talk to your Elders," Bill said, "and we'll work on ours."

"Very well," Freddy said.

"It really is lovely to see you again, Bill," Doris said. "Now that you're all grown up."

Bill blushed. He'd always liked Luke's parents. "I'm not that grown up. I'm just trying to make things right."

"Hard work, isn't it?" Freddy said.

Bill knew Freddy was no stranger to tough stuff. Though Luke's dad wasn't an Elder, it was his job to bury their dead with dignity after attacks. This was considered a high calling, and it was a duty he fulfilled with great reverence.

"Yeah. It feels never-ending," Bill said.

"Sometimes," said Freddy.

"But I'm lucky," Bill said.

His mind leapt to an image of his parents and Maia, huddled in fear against some advancing threat. And just like that, his determination returned anew.

"Lucky?" It was Omar, poking his head out from behind Felix's shadow.

"Yeah, lucky. Because I still have plenty to lose," Bill said. "Maia taught me that."

Omar recoiled slightly at the mention of Maia, while Diego nodded proudly.

"We need to find that human den, Luke," said Felix. "Can you take us there?"

"Hold on a minute," said Doris, grabbing her son and clutching him to her chest. "You're not going anywhere with our baby. We only just got him back!"

"Classic Teddycat thinking," Freddy said, shaking his head. "Our kid gets nabbed while risking his scruff on their behalf. Then he escapes by the skin of his tail, and the very next day—no kidding, the very next day—they show up with a jaguar, demanding a guided tour back to the scene of the crime!"

"Unbelievable," Doris said.

"Well, forget that," said Freddy. "Luke is staying right here. Where he belongs."

Luke struggled against his mother's tight embrace.

"He can scratch you a map," Doris said.

"Stop!" shouted Luke. "I'm going with them!"

"Oh, no you don't!" Doris said.

Luke's scrawny limbs wriggled against her grip. "And after, we can go back to Horizon Cove," he said. "It still exists!"

"Horizon Cove was razed to the ground," Freddy said, "all because of *them*. We'll never find our way back—the ravine would have closed up by now."

"But we can bring it back," said Luke. "It's still inside of us."

"Listen to your kid," said Diego. "He's smart. We need to work together."

"Don't you dare tell me that," said Freddy, the anger rushing to his eyes. "I've got scars too, you know."

Diego's haunches tightened as Felix stepped between them. Doris finally released Luke, who scrambled free and tried to reclaim some semblance of cool.

"Look," Doris said quietly. "You've got your claws and your Kingdom up in the clouds. I'm sorry you're having trouble. I am. But you're not taking my son, no matter what he thinks. And that's final."

"We understand," Felix said. "Please forgive us."

"Good luck," said Freddy, and Bill believed he was sincere. "And thanks for the moss."

"It's from my mom," Bill said.

"Thank her for me," said Freddy.

"I will," said Bill. "If I ever see her again. You know, I think you guys would really like my mom. I think you'd really hit it off."

"Maybe," said Doris. "But it's getting late. You should go while you still have some light."

Chapter 17

LUKE MADE THEM a map out of berry juice and sun-dried fronds, and the crew set off toward the human den. But despite the brief rest, Bill's pace had slowed down to something closer to that of his older companions.

"You did your best, Bill," Felix said, not for the first time.

"I just . . ." Bill said, then trailed off with a sigh.

Conflicting emotions battled in his chest. Obviously he was relieved that Luke was okay, but he still wished he had been able to convince the Olingos to join their fight then and there. Sometimes it seemed like wherever he went, there were Elders standing in the way, stubbornly refusing to admit that the world was changing and their old ways no longer worked. Add to that the news of Jack's fate, plus the heat, general jungle fray, and the wispy width of the path they were following, and Bill was having real problems placing one paw ahead of the other, much less rushing.

Suddenly, Omar let loose a high-pitched scream. "There's something in my pack!"

Diego jumped into action. "Stand very still," he said, slowly approaching Omar. He held his walking stick in front of him like a sword.

"I felt it squirm! I think it's a snake!" Omar yelled. He began spinning in wild circles. "A whipsnake! No, wait, a bushmaster! Help!"

"I *said* freeze!" Diego said. "Quit flappin' about!"

Reluctantly, Omar froze. Diego inched forward, ears straight back, then jabbed the stick into Omar's pack.

"Ow!"

Omar screamed, winched, and commenced running in circles as his bindle unfolded.

"Stop!" Bill shouted, a smile breaking his face. "It's not a snake!"

A pair of scraggly ears poked out of Omar's bindle, and then out popped a whole head. It was Luke, smiling with a mouthful of figs.

"Did you really think I was going to let you guys go without me?" he said.

Bill helped him out of the bindle, and everyone—except Omar, still recovering from his snake anxiety—greeted Luke warmly.

A party of five, they resumed their travels. Luke regaled them with the noisy drama surrounding his bold insistence on leaving the family den.

"I stood up and said, 'Mom, Dad, I'm outta here! Like it or not. It's time to rewrite Teddycat–Olingo history!'"

"Wait a minute," Bill said. "Are you sure you didn't sneak out, then hide in Omar's bindle for the last half a klick until Diego poked you with a branch?"

"I guess that's about right," Luke sniffed. "Anyway, you're welcome."

Omar was still catching his breath and trying to act casual, but Diego was unembarrassed by his vigilance. In fact, Bill thought he seemed disappointed that there hadn't been a snake strapped to Omar. But nevertheless the atmosphere was still buzzing with danger, as ever-present and tangible as the humidity, as species clashed amid a constantly shifting food chain. And maybe it wasn't the snake—or lack of a snake—that had Diego still on edge. He and Jack had been through a lot together, and Bill knew how much it had to hurt Diego to learn that he was probably gone.

"I liked what you were saying back there about Horizon Cove," Felix said to Luke.

"Aye, that was good stuff, kid," Diego said.

"Thanks," said Luke, bopping along now.

"And I think you're right," Felix said. "I think we *can* find it again."

"Where'd you learn all that stuff anyway?" Omar asked.

"Different places," Luke said. "Some of it from Bill."

"Yeah, that was good stuff, Luke," Bill said, trying to deflect any attention—or follow-up questions—Luke's praise might attract. "I almost felt like I was really there, prying our way through the ravine. Say, wanna give me a hand with my pack?"

"Quit trying to off-load your responsibilities, Bill," said Omar.

"Hey, Omar," Bill said, "there's something on your neck."

Omar started hyperventilating again, and when everybody laughed, since there was nothing *actually* there, he relaxed into a scowl.

Bill looked up. Light trickled through the canopy. Best he could tell, it was early afternoon. He could still hear the distant grumble of rushing water that had been accompanying them for quite some time, which at least provided a constant, a North Star. Every few minutes it seemed to grow louder.

"So first we go back to where Elena was taken, the same place you were taken, Luke, then find the humans from there, right?" Bill asked.

"Huh?" said Luke. "I know the way from my den, that's about it."

"But I thought your map had us following the trail from the clearing!" Bill said. "Didn't the human take you straight from the trap to the camp?"

"But I don't remember much of that trip . . ." Luke confessed. "I was scared. Everything was a blur. And there was a giant leaf or something draped over the cage!"

Bill stopped. The others followed his lead, and they all stood there in an uneven, rumpled circle. Dragonflies and other winged beasts circled their heads. Every now and then the scent of deep rot would pass through, an unwelcome reminder of the jungle's bottomless capacity to absorb life. Felix wiped grime from his face. His expression was pained but still doggedly patient.

"What is our best chance of finding the camp?" asked Felix.

"It's a straight shot from my den," said Luke.

"So we are headed in the wrong direction," said Felix.

"I'm sorry," Luke said, still confused. "I thought you guys knew where you were going."

Bill and Omar groaned. Diego bit his tongue, then spat blood on the ground.

"That was the whole point of going to your den in the first place!" Bill shouted.

"Oh, you're right, Bill," Luke said. "This is my fault. Here I was, thinking you visited my den to make peace with my family and offer your condolences because mere minutes ago you thought I was good as dead. But I guess it was all about *you*, as usual."

"A simple misunderstanding," Felix said, snuffing out the argument before Bill could fire back. "But now we will need to make excellent time in order to double back and still scout the area by nightfall."

"So we're really turning around?" Omar said. "We can't cut through?"

"You heard him. Turn it around," Diego said. "Clamp it and get to marchin'."

Omar dropped his snout to the ground and wheeled around wordlessly.

"Just be happy we figured this out when we did," Felix said. "Every little bit of time we save counts."

Bill groaned loud and long. "From now on, every step we take, I'm just going to be thinking about the time we wasted."

"At least it'll look familiar," Omar said.

"That's the spirit," said Felix.

"Jeez, Bill," Luke said. "My mom was right, you're *so grown up*."

Chapter 18

THE SKY TURNED plum-colored as the jungle fell into twilight. There was a volley of baleful moans as the moon rose. Daytime bugs cleared out to made room for the heavier, glowing nighttime bugs. It had been a long, largely silent afternoon as they retraced their steps.

The mission was not going as planned. They didn't bother disturbing the (admittedly confused) Olingos when they passed the den again, though Luke waved half-heartedly. Bill had been gritting his teeth so hard that his jaw would be sore by dinnertime. They would have to make camp and renew the search in the morning. It felt like time was slipping away, along with their chances.

He felt better after they settled down by a large, ferny stump and shared a rustle of grubs. The moon was low and fat, throwing soft silver on everything it touched. But it didn't touch everything, not way down in the underbrush, and it was hard for Bill to ignore the ceaseless squawks, rattles, and flickers. Harder, at least, than during the day. It made Bill realize just how groomed and well-managed the Kingdom had been. Cloud Kingdom, where everything had its place and everything had a name, as quiet and smooth as a mountain pond. Bill realized that, if their mission truly succeeded, there would be ripples, waves, wakes. He would need to become much more comfortable with the unknown, and the darkness, real quick.

Somehow, Bill slept. His dreams were tense and chaotic: Versions of Maia, Elena, and Jack, his parents and the Elders—even Freddy and Doris, arguing over a few clumps of sweetmoss—slipped through his subconsciousness like pawfuls of sand.

When he woke it was hot and bright, banners of blue sky between swaying limbs cackling like wind chimes. The jungle hum was friendlier, if still not exactly welcoming. Bill rubbed his eyes and yawned widely. It was one of those mornings, inside and out, that held the promise of a fresh beginning. The air was pungent, rich, and loamy. The jungle was so alive, so flowing and loaded, there was no way to imagine life outside of it.

As usual, Diego was on watch, diligently surveying the perimeter. He didn't trust anyone else to do the job. Bill brought him breakfast—berries and bark, nothing fancy, but still sure to be appreciated.

"Morning, Diego," Bill said, handing him the small meal.

"Thanks, mate," said Diego. He picked at Bill's offering, distracted by his duty. "How'd you sleep?"

"Pretty well."

"Sure sounded that way. You were snoring up a racket."

"What? No I wasn't!"

Bill didn't snore. Snoring was for old, wheezy Teddycats like Omar's father. Back when they were younger and still close, Bill would often spend the night at Omar's den, and of the handful of oddities Bill remembered about those visits—the whole place smelled like a larva-choked log, for instance—it was Omar's father's tree-shaking snores that stood out the most. Bill almost laughed, thinking about how badly he'd missed home, only a few dens away, during those restless nights at Omar's. Here he was lost in a foreign forest, claws to the wall, further from home than ever before.

"Whatever you say," Diego said with a smirk.

"So," Bill said, changing the subject, "when do you think we'll land at the human den?"

"It depends on your Olingo friend," Diego said. "But we can't be far now."

"You've scouted all over this jungle, right?"

"I've been to the river and back," Diego said. "But never this far down."

Diego finished the last of his breakfast. The sticky, ripe berries had stained his lips dark. He used the edge of a claw to clean the seeds from his teeth.

Bill admired Diego's claws. They were long, with graceful arcs that narrowed into glinting points.

"Hey, Diego?" Bill asked. "Why do you think the humans are so interested in our claws?"

Diego snorted. "Haven't you figured it out yet?"

It was hard to understand exactly what Diego was saying—his paw was still stuck in his mouth—so Bill just shook his head.

"I tell ya, mate," Diego said, finally pulling his paw from his mouth and considering his claws in the morning light, "at this point, these things are more trouble than they're worth."

"I thought the claws kept us safe," Bill said.

Growing up in Cloud Kingdom, every lesson young

Teddycats learned about claws (cleaning and sharpening techniques, situations for appropriate use, penalties for illegal unsheathing) included a long sermon on their role in the species' salvation. According to the Elders, they were not so much tools for survival as divine gifts bestowed upon the species. That certainly sounded impressive, but wasn't much for practicality.

"Sure, they've served us reasonably well in the jungle. But I reckon the humans don't want to climb trees with these babies."

Diego bared both sets of claws and held them up menacingly, just a hair away from Bill's eyes.

"Just ask Felix. The humans want to saw them off and make their little trinkets. They want these claws around their necks, and they don't care where they come from or how badly it hurts."

Bill leaned back and closed his eyes. A blast of fear filled the sudden darkness with a ghostly image: a wide field dotted with crying Teddycats, a gang of humans charging off with a smoky hoot, lugging bindles filled with bloody claws.

"I envy the Olingos," Diego said. "Helpless as they are, in some ways, those little buggers are safer than we are. Here's some advice, Garra: Want a long, peaceful life? Don't go around havin' anything the humans want."

"Yes, sir," Bill mumbled, thinking *Too late*.

He considered his own claws, smaller than Diego's but still sharp. They could get you into trouble, sure, but could they ever truly get you out of it? They were a blessing and a curse, an honor and a burden.

Diego yawned and scratched his lean frame. "Thanks for breakfast, kid."

"No problem," said Bill, his own appetite off and running.

The wind settled down and the clouds moved in. Everything wilted in the sweltering humidity. Diego explained that their proximity to the water meant increased chances of sudden, violent storms and possibly flooding.

Felix assembled the group and laid out the day. According to Luke's best guess, the human den was a straight shot down the river valley. However, they would need to make a hard choice. There was a wide, open savanna they had to cross. To skirt it would add a day to the trip that they—and Elena—could not afford. But crossing straight through would expose them to birds of prey and other predators. There would be no canopy, no coverage. It was like a frying pan.

"It's a trap," Omar said, "and we're walking right into it. I say we take the extra time and go around. What help are we to Elena or anybody if we get plucked to death?"

Everyone shivered at the thought. Death by bird was low on the list of any jungle dweller.

"No way," Bill said. "We've already wasted a day heading in the wrong direction. I say we make a break for it, cover up, and burrow down when needed."

"And how's old Felix supposed to burrow down through sand?" Diego asked. "He can barely keep up as it is."

"Or Luke, for that matter," Omar said.

"Hey, I've already been through it once before," Luke said.

"That's true," Felix said, "but that was at night and you were in shock. You probably didn't realize the danger you were in."

Luke shrugged.

"How about the river?" Bill asked.

"What about it?" Omar asked, his confidence buoyed by Diego's agreement.

"Why can't we take the river down?"

"Come on," Omar said. "Get serious."

"I *am* serious," said Bill. "Diego, is it possible?"

The old scout was silent for a moment. Then he hopped up in front of the group.

"We're here," Diego said, dropping a stone on the grass in front of him. "Got it?"

"Yup," Bill said.

"Now, according to Luke, this blasted camp is on the other side of the savanna." Diego drew a circle in front of the stone with his walking stick. "Here's the savanna."

"Looks about right," Luke said.

Diego ignored him and scratched in a squiggly line along the right side of both their position and the savanna. "Here's the river. With me so far?"

More nods.

"So we can either take our chances crossing the savanna, flank to the left, and add a day's walk, or take the river and float right down past the camp."

"You're saying it could work!" Bill said.

"It could work, sure," said Diego. "But it ain't much safer than the other routes. The river's a whole new pit of snakes."

"What are we gonna do?" scoffed Omar. "Build a raft?"

"That's exactly what we're going to do," said Felix.

Chapter

19

LUKE AND FELIX scrounged for useful materials—sticky mud, branches they could use to steer them down the river—while the Teddycats set to work with their claws. Beside them, the water, dark and immense, moved fast. Despite its far-reaching grumble, up close it was eerily quiet, almost silent. Bugs leapt and hissed across the wide surface as the current whipped along.

Bill downed a cluster of slender rubber trees while Diego hacked them into usable fractions and sliced loose fronds into binding ribbons. Meanwhile Omar organized their output into tidy piles. Bill felt reinvigorated, almost as if he were back working on the fort, before everything was turned upside down.

By midmorning they had assembled a no-frills yet river-worthy raft wide enough for the five of them, guided by a crude rudder. Luke found—tripped over, really—a large skeleton (Felix's best guess was hippo) and brought back two long, curved rib bones.

"How long is this going to take, anyways?" Omar asked nervously.

Historically, Teddycats were inexperienced swimmers, and Omar's aversion was stronger than average. He hated water and heights and had hoped his heroics would include neither.

"Depends on the current and the wind," said Bill.

"Which is Bill's fancy way of saying he hasn't got a clue," Omar sniped.

"We could land by lunch, or we could never be seen again, lost to the elements," Diego said. "No way to know until we set sail."

"Lunch?" said Luke. "There's an idea. What're we having?"

Together they straddled the bank and unceremoniously dunked half of the vessel into the current. It very nearly washed away, anchored only by Diego's claw as his legs stretched uncomfortably between the raft and the riverbank.

Tree limbs bent down to the water, some leaves

nearly brushing the surface. Bill climbed a trunk and scurried onto a limb, dropping down to the center of the raft with a backflipping flourish. Omar rolled his eyes. Bill and Diego assisted Felix aboard while Luke leapt on gleefully. It was fun for him to watch the Teddycats get so skittish around the water. Olingos had no such reservations. Even Bill, despite the showmanship, had a noticeable wobble as he waited for his river legs to materialize.

"All right, Omar," Bill said. "We're ready to push off."

"Uh, well . . ." Omar said nervously. "Maybe I could meet you guys down at the human den instead?"

"Let's go, mate," Diego said. He was still stretched between the bank and the raft, and the strain was taking its toll. His shoulders and hips twitched as the raft bobbed.

"Or I could stay here, just in case anybody came by looking for us," Omar said.

"Whatever you decide, do it quick," said Diego, groaning. The raft was beginning to slip away, the wood splintering as he tried to dig his claw deeper against the powerful current.

"Omar, we need you with us," Felix said.

"Come on, Omar!" chirped Luke. "Hop on!"

Bill sighed. It was time. "Omar, a few days ago I would have pushed you off this raft myself. But today, we're in this together. We'll keep you safe. I promise."

Omar closed his eyes, took a deep breath, and jumped on board just as the anchor of Diego's paw skidded off the bank and into the coursing water.

The current swept them up without ceremony. Diego and Bill slashed at the water with the bones, working to steer the raft into the middle of the river, where their line of vision would be least obstructed by dangling trees and the mist that stuck to the bank. After a period of hectic paddling and a few spins, they found themselves gliding swiftly down the river.

"Not bad, eh?" said Diego, one paw on the rudder.

As if on cue, a warm, soothing wind picked up, and the clouds began to break apart.

"Best part is, we'll get a jump on those humans," said Bill, giddy with excitement. "They'll never expect us coming from the river."

"A slight advantage, perhaps," said Felix, "but I'd argue the humans still have the upper hand."

"I'll take what I can get," Diego said.

"Uh, Omar?" Luke said. "Are you okay?"

Omar was rigid, his cheeks puffy, his eyes fixed on a single, distant point.

"You're looking a little green, buddy," Bill said.

"I'm fine," croaked Omar.

Felix rustled through his bindle and handed Omar a green plant. "Here, chew on this."

"What is it?"

"Just a little sprig of something," Felix said. "It'll ease the sickness."

Omar gobbled it up, and soon a deep, fragrant belch shot out of his mouth.

"Gross," said Luke.

"Thanks, Felix," Omar said. His color had improved, though it was clear he was embarrassed. "I feel much better."

Felix patted Omar's shoulder and closed his bindle.

"What other miracle cures you got in there, Felix?" asked Diego.

"That depends," said Felix. "What do you need?"

"Not sure—how about one of them trippy frogs?"

As Felix and Diego shared a laugh, Bill turned to Luke. "Keep your eyes open for anything you might recognize from your last trip."

"Well, you can almost make out the savanna," said Luke, pointing to the left bank.

The mist over there *was* looking a little thin and dusty, Bill thought.

"How big would you say the savanna is?" asked Bill.

"Gotta be several klicks," Diego said. "But then, can't say I've ever crossed it, only kicked around its borders. Not sure I've met anyone who has, until Luke here."

"Wow," said Bill, jealous that the reverence in Diego's tone was directed at Luke instead of him. "You must've been flying high on adrenaline."

"It's all a blur," Luke said dreamily.

"Still mighty impressive," Bill said.

"Um, guys, what's that?" asked Omar. He was pointing to the water, and that queasy shade of green was creeping back into his face.

Bill bounced over to the starboard edge to take a closer look.

"Easy," said Diego, as the raft pitched.

Bill could make out the vague shape of something just beneath the surface. He lowered his head and peered closer. Just then, a black coil lashed out of the water and zapped Bill's snout.

"Ahh!" cried Bill. "It bit my face! It bit my face!"

Omar laughed. "Ha ha. No it didn't."

"It's an eel," said Felix. "They're electrified."

"Get away from the water!" growled Diego.

Omar and Bill inched back to the middle. Bill rubbed his snout.

"This isn't a game, mates," Diego continued. "And the eels aren't the only ones to watch out for. Some of these fishies swimming along here will rip your flesh straight off your bones before you even know what hit ya."

To illustrate his point he jabbed the hippo rib in their direction.

"Welcome to the river, boys," said Felix. "It's a long way from Cloud Kingdom, I know, but if you pay attention you'll find there's logic and order at work here as well."

"Are there really fish that can . . . do what he said?" Omar asked.

"Yes," said Felix.

Felix had seen plenty of animals, brave and otherwise, freeze up in the jungle, too frightened to even understand the dangers they faced if they didn't fight or flee.

"All right, eel's gone," Diego said. "Now get back to the bow and keep lookout."

Chapter

 20

THE SUN WAS shining and the wind was warm at their backs as they drifted purposefully down the river. The current was quick but steady, nothing Diego couldn't handle. They had even set down their paddling bones, letting the river do the work as the water turned from a bleak brown to a sharper blue and the mist cleared.

"I could get used to this," said Bill, reclining in the sunshine.

"Have to admit," said Omar, "it sure beats humping through the jungle brush. I've got thorns and bramble cuts all over."

"You've got to learn to be one with the wilderness, my friend," Bill said.

Omar laughed. "Sounds like you've already forgotten about the swamp thing that almost stole your snout."

"Can't let that keep you down," said Bill lightheartedly.

"Stay on task," Diego warned.

Omar and Bill were supposed to be on watch duty, but they had grown drowsy with sun. The unchanging river unfurled before them, and despite its power and beauty it could not hold their attention. Luke was actually sleeping. Bill figured he might as well join his friend.

"Wake me up when we get to the human den," said Bill, yawning.

"Let's not grow complacent," Felix said. "It's calm now, but there's still plenty that can go awry."

Diego, clearly fed up with his lookouts, listed some potential dangers. "Crocs, piranhas, eddies that'll suck ya under in no time flat. Ever seen a croc up close? One of them knobby monsters could swallow this entire operation in one bite. One of them, a legendary sucker, Boris, he's got a long yellow stripe down his back. Here's hopin' you never meet him. Old Boris has chomped down whole boats of humans."

Bill and Omar exchanged glances, then quickly got back to work. It did seem like it would be best to avoid a run-in with a croc. Instead of resting, they admired the jungle from their currently peaceful vantage point. Every now and then they spotted movement in the trees—toucans, lizards, monkeys, sloths, and bands of coatis—lurking, slithering, hunting, grooming, or just making a racket high in the trees. Bill allowed himself to imagine a future where the Teddycats were integrated into jungle society. Then he would finally be allowed to wander the land, free and not beholden to any rules or Elders. They weren't there just yet, but close enough that failure would sting like never before.

They had grown so accustomed to the river's rumble that they didn't notice as it gradually grew into a roar. The current picked up as well, but at first that had seemed like a good thing. After all, they'd welcome anything that might shorten the journey. But then the raft began to list. Diego and Bill returned to paddling duty and tried to steer them back into the middle as Felix leaned against the rudder with all his diminished might.

"What's tipping us?" asked Omar, working hard to remain calm.

"Hopefully just rapids up ahead," Diego said.

"White water," whispered Luke.

"What'd you say?" Bill asked from the port side.

"White. Water!" said Luke, pointing to a frosting of sloshy caps in the near distance.

The water lashed back at them as they dug their oars into the current, trying to carve a line back on course. Soon they were spinning sideways and picking up speed. Their hippo bones sliced through the water but seemed only to accelerate their loss of control. The mist returned, thicker now, and settled smack in the center of the river valley.

"Time to consider the idea that there might be a drop ahead," said Felix.

"How big?" Diego asked.

"I can't say," said Felix, sighing. "But based on our speed and trajectory . . ."

"You're sayin' it might be a real inconvenience," said Diego.

"Something like that."

"Give me a boost," said Bill, beckoning Omar and Diego.

Startled, they complied. It took a moment to secure footing. The raft was no longer spinning, but waves had started to form as the current squeezed the water.

Omar and Diego each grabbed a paw and lifted until Bill's hindquarters were level with their snouts.

"What do ya see?" asked Diego.

Bill squinted and shielded the sun with a flattened paw. "Nothing yet."

"Jeez, you're heavy," said Omar.

Luke tried to help, but Bill's weight was awkward and not easily shared.

Felix stayed with the rudder, trying in vain to steer them to a bank. But while the river had narrowed, the trees had pulled back like a curtain. There were no longer gracefully dangling limbs within reach, just heaps of boulders. "Luke, come help me," Felix said.

Together they tugged on the rudder as Bill tried to keep his balance.

"No rush, mate!" shouted Diego, his voice nearly lost to the spray. "Anytime now!"

Bill leaned forward. The mist was like a sheet. "Let me down," he said, trampling the shoulders of his supporters.

"What did you see?" asked Diego.

"Well, I don't know how big it is, but there's definitely a drop."

The raft was straight as an arrow, pitched slightly forward. Instinctively, they began to move to the stern.

The rudder rattled violently then fell away through the wooden slats, ripped out by rocks or just the force of the current.

"If we make it through this, we're definitely sticking to land from now on," Omar said.

"Agreed," said Bill.

The roar reached a thunderous crescendo as boulders created a ripping funnel and rapids rocked the raft. Spray soaked their fur as the mist enveloped them, reducing visibility to only an immediate, increasingly panicked pocket.

"Here we go, mates," said Diego, steeling himself.

"Whatever happens," said Felix, "do not bail out! Stay on the raft!"

"Teddycats, use your claws!" Bill said. "Luke and Felix, grab on to us!"

Luke immediately latched onto Bill, all four limbs plus tail wrapped around his friend's torso like a pole. Felix went flat on his stomach and hooked two arms around Diego, who stabbed his claws into the wood as the raft launched forward.

Chapter
 21

THEY WERE ONLY airborne for a moment, but as the raft catapulted out of the mist, it stretched out into what felt like a lifetime.

Memories long forgotten swelled and turned so real Bill felt he could reach out and kiss his mother, smell Cloud Kingdom grass, feel the warmth of the straw in his den. He could hear Maia's laugh—and not that low, dry "ha" when Bill did something stupid, but the rare, lyrical cackle she couldn't control, the one that made Bill believe they knew each other even better than they could understand.

The raft kept falling. Bill could somehow sense his father holding him as a little kitten, swearing he would always protect him. Even the Elders emerged, outlined in an anxious red aura but glowing with concern, their hands outstretched in welcome. Bill could feel old judgments falling away. His frustrations flattened. A warm, vibrant space appeared—just a speck on the horizon, more of a feeling than a destination, a golden crack in the earth—and pulled at him.

The raft plunged into the water. It was cold and cloudy. They shot deep into the basin at the foot of the falls. The Teddycats held on for dear life, while Luke and Felix held on to the Teddycats. The raft scraped the bottom, where the water was dark but clear. For a terrifying moment, the force of the falling water pressed them against the sand. Bill twisted about, unsure whether to release his claw and make a break for the surface, but Felix's words—*Stay on the raft!*—stuck with him. Suddenly, the raft caught a current, which lifted them violently from the bottom and spat them out.

WHEN BILL CAME to, they were beached on a flat rock, chests heaving. He counted all four of his comrades, safe and sound, but the raft wasn't so lucky. Their river craft was destroyed, splintered and scattered, their supplies lost. The sun had baked the stone to a stinging degree, but Bill didn't want to move. At least, not quite yet. Though the waterfall was still within sight, its thunder had been silenced. There was only the throb of blood. Bill shook his head until his ears popped and the roar returned.

The rock was beginning to burn his fur. He rose, slowly, his spine creaking, and stretched his battered muscles. His neck was sore. He was dizzy. There were stars in his eyes.

"Everybody all right?" he asked, a bit unsteady on his paws.

Diego groaned. "I'm gettin' too old for this."

"I think so," said Omar, scanning his body for damage. "Just got the wind knocked out of me pretty bad."

"Glad to hear it," said Bill. "Hey, Luke, how many toes am I holding up?"

"Not now, Bill," said Luke. He was soaked and shaking, fur plastered to his bones.

"Good enough," said Bill. "How about you, Felix?"

Felix was crumpled on the rock, his injured leg at a painful angle. His spots seemed to disappear, and his eyes were closed.

"Felix?" Bill said. "Felix, are you all right?"

He rushed to the jaguar's side. His body was limp and heavy.

"Wake up, Felix!" Luke pleaded.

Diego put an ear to Felix's chest. "He's swallowed a lot of water."

"Okay, I know what to do," Bill said. "Diego, hold him steady."

Bill took a deep breath. A lancing pain shot through his lungs, but he ignored it and gathered as much air as he could hold. He peeled open the droopy flaps that hung over Felix's jaw. The exposed fangs were gleaming and rigid, but in his resting mouth they seemed more like decoration than powerful weapons. Bill blew forcefully into the jaguar's mouth, then pumped away at his chest while Diego held Felix's head in his lap and spoke softly into his ear.

Bill's father had taught him how to resuscitate an injured animal when he was very young. He had even practiced on a bed of straw wrapped in leaves. *Always be prepared* was his father's motto, and though Bill had never used the technique before on a living creature, he found himself right back at home with his father, the bundle of straw dying on the floor of the den.

He listened for a heartbeat but heard nothing. Another deep, lung-cracking breath; another round of chest presses; more tender coaxing from Diego.

Omar and Luke watched in silence.

"Come on, mate," Diego urged.

Bill took one last breath. He tried to capture all the power of the jungle, the gratitude and friendship in his heart, their collective need for Felix's dignity and quiet strength. He couldn't imagine accomplishing their mission without him. Bill would carry him the rest of the way if that's what it took. The air was bruising—it made his eyes water. He blew every last particle into Felix's lungs, then pounded his chest.

One! Two! Three! Four!

Suddenly, a spout of water shot out of Felix's mouth and splashed Bill in the face.

Everyone leapt back as Felix gargled for a moment, spat out another lungful of water, and rolled over onto his side with a groan. Slowly, he turned back over, eyes open.

"Felix, you're alive!" exclaimed Bill.

Omar, Luke, and even Diego whooped in celebration.

Felix smiled, dazed and maybe slightly embarrassed. "Are we there yet?"

Chapter

IT WAS A good question.

With the raft destroyed, their food and tools lost to the drink, and nobody in much of a rush to get back on the water, the crew set about figuring their position. Luke and Omar gathered whatever foodstuffs they could find on the riverbank—mostly bland grass and slugs— while Diego tried to salvage what he could from the raft. There was very little left over, though he did manage to fashion a new prowling stick from one of the splintered hippo bones found washed up down the bank.

Bill sought high ground, as was his nature. He climbed a series of boulders, trying to calculate their distance from the savanna and, with any luck, the human den. He couldn't get too high—the waterfall's mist obscured the view—but he eventually hopped from a wet rock formation to an umbrella tree. He climbed the trunk until it began to bend, then took in the vista.

To the west was the waterfall. Bill shook his head. It seemed insane that they had survived. It looked like a longer drop than the fall on the side of Cloud Kingdom, long considered a death sentence by Teddycats and featured in tragic jungle legends. To the east lay the continued arc of the river. It was impossible to see past the next bend. The savanna was straight ahead, flat and dusty. It appeared they had landed deep in the savanna. There was a thick but finite chunk of green between the dust bowl and what Bill hoped was the dent of the river valley.

He sighed and counted his blessings. Everyone was alive. The fresh air felt good—the humidity, once heavy and bothersome, now tasted sweet to his tongue and cool on his lungs—and carried the scent of fresh rain and breadfruit blossoms. Across the river, just before the bank slid into the savanna, there stood a huge tree, twisted and gnarly. Bill decided to cross the river and climb the giant. Hopefully the view from the top would confirm the edge of the savannah and lead them the rest of the way to the human den.

BILL SAUNTERED BACK to the group, his eyes slightly glassy. He was still riding high off Felix's recovery and their miraculous survival. Every now and again a shiver would slither down his spine, a reminder of the sheer fact that he was alive. Bill thought it might be best if he *always* felt this way—grateful, full of wonder and appreciation—and he pledged to dedicate more time to reflection as soon as this was all over and Elena was safe.

"Find anything useful?" Diego asked.

"Not much," Bill said. "You?"

"Eh." Diego shrugged, nudging a pile of scraps. "Not that we had a lot to begin with . . ."

"Now there's a bright side for you," said Bill. "We're no longer weighed down with pesky supplies. Luke and Omar, how goes the hunting and gathering?"

"Depends," Omar said. "If you like mudslugs, it's an all-you-can-eat buffet."

"A Teddycat cannot live on mudslugs alone," Bill mused. "But they'll have to do for now. Felix, feeling any better?"

"Much improved, thank you," Felix said, with an upturned grimace. "I saw you climbing—any idea where we are?"

Bill relayed the sights while choking down a scoop of muddy slugs. He tried not to oversell the prospects. It was only a tree in a jungle full of them, but it was better than nothing.

"And you think this tree is promising?" Felix asked.

"It's our only lead," said Bill. "But it's closer to the savanna, and it might let us see which way the river snakes. With any luck it'll point us in the right direction."

"Then I suppose we cross the river and hope for the best," said Felix.

"*Snakes?*" said Luke.

Chapter

 **23**

ONCE FELIX ASSURED the group that he was recovered enough to move, they humped across the river, arm in arm, through the edge of the basin's shallow water and slack current. Just downriver, before the bend, was another series of rapids, which reminded them all of their reasons for abandoning water travel for dry land.

"If I had to get chewed up, I'd choose a big cat to do it," said Diego more or less out of nowhere. "Death by croc is the absolute worst way to go."

"Is that right?" said Bill, trying not to imagine either scenario.

"Any day," Diego said. "Less messy, for starters. Just ask Felix."

"No thanks," said Omar.

"Hey, Felix," said Diego, unwilling to drop the subject, "you and your cat cousins are dainty eaters, yeah?"

"We're *respectful*," Felix said. "By and large."

"That's all you can ask for these days," said Diego. "Just a spot of respect. Not like what these *humans* are offering."

"Amen," said Omar.

They fished one another out of the water and shook themselves dry. Up close, the tree was even more massive than Bill had imagined. The roots alone dwarfed him. They stretched and folded like boas across the wide, grassy clearing that had developed in the tree's expansive ring of shade. It was the biggest tree he had ever seen. While the others offered encouragement, Bill heaved himself up a gnarled root, scampered to the vast trunk, and began to climb.

The bark was deeply grooved, making it easy to snag a claw, but Bill's limbs were still sore from the underwater thrashing. The tree seemed to go on and on. By the time he reached the first significant offshoots, a certain dizziness returned. He was not yet high enough to oversee the savanna, so he put his snout to the trunk and forced himself not to look down.

On the rare occasion when Bill felt outmatched by a climb, he narrowed his focus to the few inches right in front of him. The color of the bark was a rich, chocolate brown. It smelled old and nutty. Bill thought about how long the tree had been there and what it must have survived as the jungle grew and changed around it. He remembered what Felix had said about seasons, and the long life cycles of the jungle. Countless plants had been suffocated, strangled by darkness, as the enormous tree grew over hundreds of years.

Bill could no longer hear the shouts of encouragement coming from below. The air thinned. He was high enough to see over the surrounding area, but not through the shimmering mass of the tree's foliage. Bill dug in and kept climbing. His fur was dry, stripped by the altitude. Finally, the trunk began to narrow, and the upper limbs were slender enough to provide a glimpse through the leaves. He reached a sturdy nub and inched his way away from the trunk. He could see all the way to the savanna and the surrounding forests; in the distance, the slowly bending river. From that height, it all seemed very peaceful. Bill felt a pang of homesickness. But then, suddenly, he saw something: puffs of dark gray clouds, but not in the sky. It was coming from the earth, drifting up through the trees. He hooted with relief and delight.

"I see something!" Bill yelled down. "I think it's the humans!"

His words echoed across the jungle. He took one last look, savoring the triumphant view, and then began his descent.

BACK IN THE shady clearing, Bill reported his findings.

"Huge plumes of weird gray clouds coming up from the earth, from the edge of the savanna," he said. "Does that jibe with what you saw, Luke?"

"Well, they *did* have a huge fire," said Luke, shuddering as he remembered the humans' cold-blooded carousing as their captives cried throughout the night. "I think there were dark clouds spewing up from it, but it was hard to see . . ."

"This feels right," said Bill, rubbing his paws together in anticipation.

He was trying not to get too far ahead of himself. They had already been through so much that it seemed impossible they might finally be this close. But as the excitement chased away his lingering fatigue and got the crew back in shape, it was hard not to feel like they were close to finding Elena and starting the trip back home.

"Wow," said Omar. "Maybe that crazy river dropped us off exactly where we need to be."

"Stranger things have happened, mate," Diego said.

Felix was quiet, barely reacting to Bill's news. The waterfall and near-drowning had obviously taken a toll. He was shivering, unable to get warm despite the heat and exertion, and he still wore the same dazed, peaceful expression. His spots were fading. Bill thought back to when he first met Felix, and his condition in Cloud King-dom. Back there it had been hard to see Felix as truly sick. But Bill saw now that Felix's patience, generos-ity, and decency might have made him appear stronger than he was. It had never been just his leg. Felix was old, ill, and yet he had chosen to leave the safety and comfort of Cloud Kingdom despite all that. Bill was determined not to fail him.

"What do you think, Felix?" asked Omar.

"Well, if those clouds are coming from a fire, then that almost certainly means humans," said Felix.

"We can skirt the savanna and make it by dusk," said Bill excitedly. "Luke and I will lead the way. Diego and Omar, help Felix. This is our shot, guys. Let's make it count."

Chapter

WIND BLEW IN from the savanna, leaving dust on their tongues and in their eyes. Bill wished he still had his bindle so he could secure it over his snout. The others were having an even worse time. Felix was wheezing. Omar and Diego had to stop every few minutes to hold him as he hacked violently into his paw. Bill tried to ignore these painful sounds and focus on their destination. There were signs everywhere pointing to the humans: foreign litter, jagged and shiny wreckage, grooved and gaping tracks that spanned the width of the jungle paths, that sharp smell. The human mark on the jungle became glaringly obvious as they grew closer to the source of the gray cloud.

Bill could still see the plume. It was one of those things that, once seen, became very hard to unsee. Every shaft of sunlight seemed discolored, every cloud disturbed. A sense of rue and violation permeated the wild. Everything was unnaturally still, the wildlife driven deep into hiding, as if waiting for the humans to take what they wanted and leave.

But what if they never left? What if they never got enough? Bill imagined the humans were at least as stubborn as the Elders, so if they really wanted something, they had no trouble ignoring everything else to get it. Still, Bill was excited to see the humans. He also believed, secretly, perhaps even subconsciously, that the jungle would reward his bravery and determination, that in the end it would grant victory to those who had always been there, those who called the jungle home and treated it respectfully.

Bill and Luke acted as scouts, blazing the trail. Every now and then Luke would point out something foreign left behind by the humans. Metal husks, shards made of a sharp translucent substance, deep tracks. Suddenly, somebody was calling Bill's name. He turned around. It was Omar, running to catch up.

"We've got to stop," Omar said, breathing hard.

"We're so close," Bill said. He knew that Felix was in pain, but he also believed that Felix would want them to reach the humans—and Elena—as quickly as possible. "Once we get within sight of the den we'll take a break and plan our next move. Sound good?"

"Yeah, sounds great, Bill," Omar said peevishly, "but Felix can barely walk. He can barely *breathe*. We have to slow down if he's going to make it the rest of the way."

Bill stared at the ground and rubbed his snout. "What does Diego say?"

"He agrees with me," said Omar. "Bill, we have to stop."

"We're so close," Bill whined. "Once we find the humans, Felix will have plenty of time to rest. Let's keep up the momentum."

"How do you know that?" said Omar. "What if we need to grab Elena right away? What if she's hurt?"

"You know, you're right," Bill said, puffing his chest and trying not to lose his cool. "I have no idea how this will actually turn out. Happy now? But I'm here for Elena, and I can't wait any longer. You've seen the humans' litter; you've seen the tracks. We're so close. Slow down if you need to, but Luke and I are going on ahead."

"Um, Bill," Luke said. "I know you're excited, but maybe we should rest for a while."

"But we could be there any minute!" said Bill.

Omar sighed.

"Just give me this," Bill said, lowering his voice. "I know you haven't trusted me for a long time, Omar, and I'm sorry that we grew apart, I'm sorry that I wanted Maia all to myself, and I'm sorry that I never stood up for you. But please, push the old guy just a little more."

Omar seemed unconvinced and slightly embarrassed.

"Come on," Bill said. "Of course I care about Felix. He might not even be alive if not for me."

"Okay," Omar sighed. "I'll let him know we're close."

"Thank you, Omar. We *are* close, I promise. I can feel it."

THE FIRE LUKE mentioned was still smoldering, those thick clouds rising from a pile of charred wood, blackened tangles of twigs, and more of those sharp and metallic shards the animals encountered along the way. The ashes had scattered across the den and settled in the swirls of mud and freshly severed tree stumps. Luke and Bill wandered the wreckage, waiting for the others to arrive, shaking their heads in disbelief.

"This was the place," said Luke. "I guarantee it. I can still smell them."

It was true that the site had a lingering, ghostly presence, but there were no signs of Elena or Jack, no traps or cages, no bones or graves.

"I don't understand," Luke said. "Where did they go?"

Bill felt awful. He was not looking forward to the arrival of the rest of the gang, who had been carrying Felix for so many klicks, pushing him along because Bill had promised that they were close to finding Elena. But their best lead—Bill's lead—had led them only to an abandoned den. Now the humans could be anywhere. They could be marching to Cloud Kingdom at that very moment. Bill had thought his insistence on speed was a sign of leadership, a hard decision made for the greater good of the mission, but standing in the ashes now, it felt more like a reckless tantrum. They had dashed through the jungle and nearly drowned, all for nothing.

He turned away from Luke. He didn't want his best friend to see his tears of guilt and frustration. A shudder of helplessness fluttered in his chest and pinched his brain. His ears were flat, his claws dull and useless. He would have to apologize to Felix, and he would have to find another way to save Elena and Jack, but he was all out of ideas.

Chapter

 25

FELIX AND DIEGO took the bad news calmly. Omar was steaming mad at first, but he swallowed his rage once he saw Bill's slumped shoulders and wet eyes. Together the group walked the site, searching for clues. There were scratches and divots in the mud; a couple of smelly leather contraptions shaped like a human's paw; a pile of golden husks that Felix identified as part of a human weapon; and a menacing, claw-like blade stuck in a tree.

The whole time, Bill half-expected the humans to return. The air felt occupied. He didn't feel safe, even though it was clear they were gone.

Felix motioned for the gang to take a seat around the gray fire pit. "I know you all are disappointed," he said once everyone had gathered.

Bill felt his snout heat up with remorse, and he stared down at his paws. Felix looked very tired. He shouldn't have pushed him so hard. He should have listened.

"It has been a long journey, and we still have a ways to go," Felix continued. "But this is the jungle—things can change in an instant! Some of you already know that. Others are still learning. Yes, the humans were here. We can smell them and see their fire and the mess they left behind."

He gestured to the debris.

"This is all useful. Their arrogance and lack of respect makes them easy to find. Despite our best efforts we did not get here in time, but we will find them. In the jungle we learn to adjust and adapt. Sometimes the current is fast and smooth; other times it drops you off a cliff. The secret to success—and survival—is a willingness to keep moving forward. The humans have moved on? Great—so will we."

"I'm sorry," Bill said. "I got too excited and I didn't consider the safety of the group. I just saw the cloud and chased after it."

"Your passion is an asset," said Felix, his voice soothing as balm.

"You did what ya thought was right," Diego said. "Besides, I couldn't have climbed that crazy tree. Couldn't even see the top!"

"It *was* pretty tall," said Bill, sniffling.

"So where do we go now?" asked Omar.

"That depends," Felix said. "Luke, you're *sure* this is the site where you were held?"

"I'm positive," Luke said.

Felix limped past the fire to the deep ruts in the mud. The tracks seemed to head in both directions—to the river and to the savanna. He knelt down and sniffed the tracks. "If the humans went to the river, then there will be no way to track them. But in the savanna they will be exposed. If we follow them through, day and night, we will find them."

"Does that mean they're headed to Cloud Kingdom?" asked Omar.

The group exchanged anxious glances.

"That's not important now," Felix said. "What matters is *our* next move."

"That's what my father always says," Bill said.

"Well, it's true," Felix said. "Now let's see if we can use anything they left behind."

THEY DUMPED MUD onto the fire until the gray clouds turned white and wispy before finally getting snuffed out. This made Bill feel better. The sun was shining. The savanna was only a short ridge away, and the humans were sure to leave a trail in the dirt. Omar had forgiven him, and Felix still believed in their mission. All was not lost. Just another temporary setback. He was still a little embarrassed by his tears. If any of the group had noticed them, Bill hoped it was interpreted as a sign of his dedication, rather than immaturity. Besides, maybe he felt better now *because* of the tears. They had been a release. Also, hadn't he pledged to be honest with himself and his friends? This was the real Bill Garra, flaws and all. He could squeeze out a few tears whenever he felt the need. Still, he wanted to apologize once more to Felix. And probably Omar.

"Don't worry about it, Bill," Omar said, combing the tall grasses on the outskirts of the campsite, searching for lunch.

Everyone was hungry, and the savanna was certain to be a dead zone, meal-wise.

"I really did mean what I said back there," Bill said. "About us and all."

"Right," said Omar, head still in the grass.

"I just got too caught up in the rescue, and I lost sight of the most important thing: our own safety. After all, like you said, what good are we to Elena if we're too exhausted to move?"

"Exactly."

The fact that Omar was speaking to him at all was a good sign, but there was something funny—stiff—in his tone, and he seemed very preoccupied with whatever was hiding in the grass.

"So," Bill said, drawing the discussion out, "we're okay?"

"We're fine, Bill."

Bill looked up from Omar and surveyed the site. The jungle was already reclaiming it, curling about the edges, erasing the damage the humans had caused. "Hey," said Bill, "remember when Maia carved 'PET ME' in your fur?"

Omar didn't say anything, but Bill caught the early curl of a smile.

"Let's just get back to work."

"Sure," said Bill. "See you out there."

Felix was more gracious about Bill's apology, maybe because he was older, or maybe because he was just too tired to put up a fuss. Whatever it was, he seemed more concerned with Bill's well-being and emotional fortitude.

"You're a good kid," he said. "Don't forget that, no matter what happens."

Bill was surprised at how much better the jaguar's words made him feel.

THE RIDGE BETWEEN the forest and the savanna was short but steep. Together the crew pushed their way up the incline.

Diego had found a new stick, Luke was whistling, Omar kept mum but was moving along. Meanwhile, Bill was completely focused on the bright side: This new direction meant that they were already on the way back to Cloud Kingdom. They were going home, and it was only a matter of time until they had Elena back and Maia could finally forgive him.

He was also happy to be leaving the human site behind. While it was true he was still on their trail, in their wake, the tattered remains of their squat had made Bill uneasy. It was not a place he knew or understood, and it had an effect on him, a certain bitterness on his tongue, smoke in his eyes, ears and fur at an odd angle. The jungle was not meant to look that way, flattened and whipped, cut down and burned to a crisp. On the ridge they were back in the lush green, fragrant and chaotic and maddeningly dense.

Secretly, Bill was holding out hope that they would see the humans from the crest, somewhere in the near distance, kicking up dust. He tried to temper that expectation. The air had cleared, smoke and grievances extinguished. No reason to get fired up all over again. Felix's encouraging words stayed with him. Bill hoped this meant that he was truly becoming a member of the jungle, able to communicate meaningfully with other species, applying special Teddycat skills to the problems of others. It was hard to believe how deep they had traveled in just a few days. Bill used to think the Olingo den was really out there. He had never entered the savanna, much less crossed it. But these were the types of valuable experiences he could bring to the Elders in an effort to demonstrate the possibilities of life down below. Bill hacked at a web of vines. It felt good to make things a bit easier for those behind him.

He turned, and there was Luke, right beside him. "Feels good to get out of there," Bill said. "I can't imagine how it must've been for you."

"So now you understand why I couldn't draw a map?" said Luke.

"I do, buddy," said Bill. "Humans are disorienting. One more reason we have to stick together."

A final threshold of brush separated them from the crest. Bill flailed his arms, shredding a path through the thicket.

"Bill, hold on!" Omar shouted. "It's Felix!"

Felix was lying on his side, his head cradled in Diego's forelegs. That dazed and peaceful expression had returned to his face. His eyes were clear but narrowed, as if he barely had the energy to keep them open, and though his body seemed to have shrunken in size, it also seemed to be embraced by an aura of peace.

"What's the matter?" Bill asked, rushing over to Felix's side. "What's wrong? Did something bite you? Is it your leg?"

"Nothing's wrong," Felix said. "I'll be fine."

He wheezed, that same sickening sound Bill had tried to outrun while chasing the smoke.

"We'll rest here for a bit," said Bill. "There's no rush."

"Nonsense," said Felix. "You all go on ahead. I'll catch up with you."

"No way," said Bill. "Right, guys?"

"No way," agreed Omar. "We need you, Felix."

"We need you!" Luke said.

But Diego was silent.

"Where would we be without you?" Bill whispered.

"I'll be right behind," Felix said softly. "You all run ahead. Remember the seasons. And if you get lost, just look to the horizon, the last line of light."

"We're not leaving you here," Bill said. "I won't do it!"

Omar and Luke dropped their heads. Even Bill knew his protests were futile. This was the jungle. There was no outrunning it, no way to hide. Eventually, the jungle came for everyone.

"You must," Felix said. "I insist."

Suddenly, a tranquil harmony closed in around them. A delicate composition of soft air, whispering wind. The sounds of the wild, the rustle of leaves. The color of the sky, the shapes of the clouds. Flickering light and shadows. It was as if the fierce, feral jungle paused for a moment just to reassure them of its balance.

"Go on," Felix urged. His eyes were pale slits, but they held no fear. Bill felt a spirit pass through the group, like a warm stream, pooling in their chests and delivering a deep sadness that somehow also promised peace. "You'll be great."

The warmth swelled and radiated until it was almost too much to bear, and then it was gone, re-absorbed by the surrounding wilderness.

Chapter

26

THEY DIDN'T CELEBRATE when they broke through the brush and reached the crest. Before them, the savanna stretched for days. They scanned for telltale dust clouds and human caravans, but saw only a long slog with no shade or water. Nobody wanted to be the first to leave the shade of the jungle and slide down into the blinding yellow sand.

Something else tugged at them as well. The ridge was still home to Felix. Leaving meant they would be forced to say a final farewell.

Bill slicked back his fur, grimed with dusty sweat, and turned to the others.

"We left behind a good friend," Bill said, his voice clogged with gratitude and sorrow. "And all we can do now is try to live up to his example. The humans are somewhere out there, and they have Elena. It won't be easy, but worthwhile missions rarely are, right, Diego?"

"Tough as a croc's tooth, most often," Diego said.

"Right," Bill said. He had never touched a croc's tooth and hoped he never would. "It will be hot and dry on the savanna, so we'll bring along whatever supplies we can carry. We will conserve our energy and resources while making the best time possible. At night the temperature will drop; we'll scrounge for food then."

They gathered fronds and stuffed one with bitter and hopefully worm-filled clumps of decaying under-brush. They helped one another lash the leaves to their backs, like turtle shells.

"Are we ready?" Bill asked. The band of explorers before him looked beaten down and slightly ridiculous, but there was an unmistakable determination to their grim nods of assent. "Okay. Let's go make Felix proud."

THAT DETERMINATION BEGAN to wane almost immedi-ately. The savanna was endless and excruciating. And there was something else, something beyond the heat and fatigue. Bill could not shake the feeling that they were being followed. He even entertained the idea that it was Felix's spirit, watching over them. But whenever he stopped and turned he could see nothing. The sun was blinding—the ridge was already just a dark smudge in the distance—but every few minutes Bill would swing around, absolutely sure that something was there, only to see nothing but an expanse of wiggling air.

Sweat stung Bill's eyes. His paws were fried, and his bones felt hollow, his muscles like jelly. The only thing that kept him moving was the thought of Maia's heartbreak and Felix's sacrifice, which propelled him forward despite his growing terror.

Even Diego, that stoic, battered veteran, had begun complaining about the brutal elements. "It's too hot, mates," said Diego. "We're gonna turn to crisps out here."

His dissent was contagious. Soon Luke requested a ride on Bill's back, and Omar threatened to turn around.

"There's nothing back there for you, Omar," Bill said. "We're wasting time we don't have even talking about it."

"But we're not going to make it," Omar insisted.

"Hey," Bill said, stopping short. The hard, dry dirt sizzled on his paws. "You wanted to be a hero? This is the moment, right here. We have to keep moving. Felix believed in us. He believed we could do it. And Luke, you've crossed this stretch before. Tell him it's possible."

Luke looked pained, but complied. "I've done it. It's possible. We can do it."

While not exactly rousing, Luke's speech seemed to do the trick. Diego and Omar piped down, and Bill did his best to ignore the growing, itchy sensation that they were being watched as their supposed destination seemed to bleed further and further into the distance.

Their grit and persistence was finally rewarded with a cloud in the sky. And not just any cloud—a fat, roiling, dark gray monstrosity that blocked the sun and cooled the savanna for a merciful span of late afternoon. They took advantage of this spot of good fortune by scurrying with increased vigor, stopping only briefly to nibble or catch their breath.

"I'd do anything for a juicy bite of sweetmoss," said Diego, choking down another clump of grubby mud.

Bill tried to remember the time, not that long ago, when Diego was an almost unknowable Cloud Kingdom fixture, this larger-than-life warrior scout on the front lines of defense. Now he was just another hungry Teddycat lost in the jungle, trying to hold on.

"I want to gorge myself on fruit," Omar said. "Just chop down a whole grove and go nuts."

"I miss Felix," Luke said.

"We all do, buddy," said Bill.

"He knew he wouldn't make it across this cursed sand," said Diego. "And he knew we wouldn't make it with him. The Teddycats owe him a great debt."

Everyone was silent for a moment, heavy with memories of Felix.

"Bill, do you think we'll make it?" asked Omar, breaking the silence with his quiet query. "I mean, really make it, all the way back home."

"Depends what you mean by 'home,'" Bill said. "I can't know what the Elders will say or what the rest of Cloud Kingdom will decide, but the beauty of the wilderness and the love of friends like Felix makes me realize that the jungle was our home all along. So here's the deal: First we free Elena, then we free the rest of the Teddycats."

The cloud shifted. Sunlight began to leak through the seams, and heat hovered in the air once again. They had to get back on the trail before it returned in full force.

"We're burning shade," Bill said.

"I'll go a bit further," Diego said. "For Felix."

"For Elena and Maia," said Omar.

"Let's do it," said Luke.

Bill smiled. "Take the lead, buddy."

At last, dusk came. They combed the sand for dinner as the sun settled into the distant hills and the sky faded purple. Bill's optimistic estimate placed them a little over halfway across the savanna, and no closer to catching the humans than they had been back at the ridge. Their limbs were sore, their paws tender and crusted. Bill took one last look, still haunted by the creepy sensation of strange eyes drilling into his back.

Chapter

 27

BILL WOKE WITH a chilly jostle. At first it felt like a freak cold front rushing through the savanna, brushing his body with stark wind. But then a dreaded metallic scent filled his snout, and his predicament came into sharper focus: He was trapped, surrounded on all sides by steely mesh. And then there was a second dreaded scent that told him, without question, that a human was at the handle.

His suspicions had been right all along. They *were* being followed! If only he had trusted his instincts. If only he *had* instincts! Once again his anger at the Elders reared its head. Life in Cloud Kingdom had softened his body and dulled his senses. No wonder the rescue mission had been one disaster after another. No wonder Felix was gone. Now there would only be three of them left, forced to fend for themselves in arid, hostile territory.

Bill hurled his body against the cage. He saw that he was still at the site that they'd settled for the night. He could see Luke and Omar begin to stir. Diego was a heavy sleeper—he could snooze right through an earthquake.

"Luke! Omar!" Bill hissed. "The humans—"

He froze mid-sentence. The last thing he wanted was for the humans to find his friends, too. Just because he was in a tight spot didn't mean they were *all* finished.

"What's going on, Bill?" Omar said, still sluggish after a scattered sleep.

"Stay away," Bill whispered urgently. "Lay low!"

Luke's eyes snapped open and immediately filled with fright. "Bill! What do we do?"

There was no time. Suddenly, Bill was up in the air. The human had lifted the cage. Bill tried to stay steady as the steel beneath him began to pitch. His friends were frantic.

"We'll find you, Bill!" Luke screeched.

"Just hang on!" said Omar.

Diego finally woke and, after a quick read of the situation, clamped paws over Omar and Luke's gaping mouths and tucked down behind a tuft of coarse desert grass.

Already Bill felt far away. He wanted to believe that he would see his friends again, that things would be all right in the end, but then he thought about Jack and all the troubles they had already struggled to overcome. It didn't seem like there could be much luck left over.

"Just remember what Felix said!" Bill shouted as the human, faceless and impossibly strong, carried him away.

BILL HAD NEVER been locked up before. He missed his family—his mother's endless tenderness, his father's stirring, steadfast stoicism—but he wouldn't want them to see him this way, helpless and scared.

Through the steel, he realized that they'd reached the edge of the savanna. His captor's long legs and quick stride had brought them back to the jungle faster than he could have even imagined. *No wonder we couldn't catch the humans*, he thought, slumped haplessly in a corner of the cage.

The mission felt doomed. He had been forced to abandon his friends, leaving them high and dry. Bill curled up as the cage swayed, careful not to flash a claw.

Bill was looking for landmarks, trying to memorize the human's route as they continued through the jungle. He was already planning an escape, collecting intelligence. There was no way he would meet Jack's same fate. He hadn't come this far to fall prey to the same greasy, stomping devils that snatched Elena, junked the jungle, and seemed hell-bent on ruining everything. A part of him couldn't wait to see Joe again, face to face. He would rip the ivory from Joe's neck, the gold from Joe's teeth, the fur and skin from Joe's shoulders and feet.

The human was breathing hard as they approached a clearing. Then, Bill's eyes grew wide as he saw what was inside the clearing. A glowing white orb, surrounded by smaller outposts, all bustling with activity. He had never seen anything like it. It was noisy. The whine of bright lights and the hum of cold air. Above all, a loud, constant grinding sound. Bill scanned the premises for familiar human sights—the fire pit, unnatural debris, rusted metal husks—but this human den was tidy and sleek.

The human set the cage down outside one of the smaller structures, a shiny box on stilts, and released its grip on the handle. Bill surprised himself by feeling abandoned. The unknown future felt certain to be far worse. His father had even warned him once, how creatures learn to love their captors. Bill had never understood that—especially given the way his father fought for the Elders—until now.

More humans crisscrossed the clearing. They were shrouded in some kind of bright white material, and their faces were hidden by veils of some kind of mossy mesh that was attached to coverings on their heads. Bill recognized a smell from the last human site, though not as sharp as before. And there was no smoke, no fire. What had the humans become since they left their last post? Bill's panic bloomed once more. The cage seemed to contract around him. The urge to flee was so strong, concentrated in the tense muscles of his shoulders, that he thought he might be able to plow straight through the steel bars. But when he tried, all he got was a sore snout.

The human—*his* human—returned and picked the cage back up. Bill was disappointed by the wave of relief that washed over him. Together they climbed the steps to the box, and the human opened it and went inside.

The interior was washed with white light. Bill blinked. More cages. The human unlatched Bill's and ushered him into a larger one. There was a vessel of food on the floor, and water dripped from some kind of suspended container, attached to the walls of the cage. Bill offered an unconvincing snarl in return as the human locked the new cage and walked away.

Bill hadn't had anything approaching a real meal in days, so maybe his taste was distorted, but the water was warm but clean; the food dry but surprisingly tasty. He dug in.

When the food was all gone and the resulting fog of gratitude lifted, he took stock of his surroundings. The white room was lined with cages containing animals of all stripes and sizes. Most were snoozing or otherwise silent. Bill recognized the quiet from other dull, desperate situations. He didn't expect instant camaraderie, just felt like making his presence known.

"Uh, does anybody know where we are?" he asked.

"Hi, Bill!" said a chipper voice.

Bill's head shot up. There, in the cage directly across from him, was Elena.

Chapter

 28

BILL'S BRAIN WENT blank for a moment, as white and empty as the long bright light that ran the length of the room's ceiling. As the daze faded, his focus zoomed in on Elena's tiny face, squeezed between the bars of her cage and seemingly unscathed.

"Elena, you're alive!"

"Oh, Bill, I'm so happy to see you!"

The familiar giddiness of her voice sent a spike of pleasure up Bill's spine. He couldn't believe it! Just when he thought all was lost, Elena was found. But what good was he to her now? How could he help if they were both in cages? Bill decided to leave that for later. Elena was alive and well. That was a good enough start.

"You wouldn't believe it, Elena," Bill said. "I told the Elders we had to find you, so we left Cloud Kingdom. We've been all over the jungle. We got lost, we went over a waterfall, we found a human den, and then Felix . . . well, Felix's gone."

Bill paused for a moment to catch his breath. "But I knew we'd find you, Elena. The humans caught me in the savanna, and for a second I thought it was all over, but here you are!"

"Here I am," said Elena, smiling.

Bill wondered why she was in such good spirits. Luke's account of human imprisonment had been dark and brutal, but Elena didn't seem injured or mistreated. Maybe she was too young to realize the danger she was in; maybe she didn't know what the humans were after.

He pressed on, babbling with relief. "Don't worry, we're going to get out of here. I promised your family I would get you back, and I stand by my promises. I don't care how many cages they trap us in, we're getting out of here, and then we'll bring the rest of the Teddycats someplace safe. You'll see, Elena. Things are looking up!"

"Okay, Bill," she said.

He had forgotten how young Elena was. She was just a baby. Still, there were things he needed to know from her.

"I have to ask you some questions, Elena," he said, his voice slower and softer. "How long have you been here?"

"I fell down!" Elena said.

"I know! I was there. Boy, that was scary! I'm so glad you're okay. Now, have the humans been giving you enough to eat?"

"The food here is good!" Elena said.

"Yeah, it's not half bad, is it?" Bill murmured.

He wasn't getting a lot of useful information, but he decided to try one last time. The first step toward escape was figuring out the humans' schedule. "Speaking of that, when do the humans bring the food and water? Think really hard, Elena. When do they go to sleep?"

Elena looked confused.

"Okay," Bill said. There would be more time to pry. Maybe too much time. "Never mind that for now. Do you have any friends here?"

"Of course she does," said a low, loopy voice.

Bill twisted his head, hopeful yet wary. "Who said that?"

HENRI WAS A hulking spider monkey with a wise tenor that reminded Bill of Felix. His tail curled up behind him, instinctively looped around an invisible branch. As the longest-serving facility inmate, he organized a mini-orientation so Bill could meet the others.

"All right now," Henri said. "When I say your name, introduce yourself to our new friend."

There was a general clucking of consent.

"Duffy," said Henri.

Silence.

"*Duffy,*" Henri said again.

"He's sleeping," another voice said.

"He was just up," said Henri, annoyed.

The voice dropped to a whisper. "I think he's narcoleptic."

"Duffy!"

Henri had a stern, caretaker's shout, the kind that bolted through the air like lightning. Bill had been on the receiving end of more than a few of those.

"Who?" a new voice said. "What?"

"Say something about yourself," said Henri.

Duffy was a sloth, sweet and slow. The whispering

gossip was Miguel, a small frog, apologetically poisonous and rippled with wild colors. There was also Vic, a sneering vampire bat; a snooty ocelot named Edgar; and finally, Coco, an aloof macaw.

At last it was Bill's turn to break the ice.

"Well, I don't really know where to begin," Bill said. "Elena was snatched by a human, and a gang of us formed a search party. I had just about given up when I was snatched myself, and here we are, reunited at last."

"Funny how that works out," Henri said. "Allow me to extend a warm welcome."

"Thanks," Bill said. "But I won't be here long. Elena and I are going to bust out."

The other animals laughed.

"Good luck to you both," Henri said, after the screeching and hooting subsided.

"So what kind of place is this?" Bill asked, ignoring the sarcasm. "Elena wasn't able to tell me much."

"She hasn't been here long," Henri said. "And they've treated her well so far. But . . ."

"But what?"

"Well, we've all got something the humans want. Once you figure out what that is, the writing's on the wall. Some of us are exotic pets. Others are trophies. Others possess properties that could be used as weapons."

"Sorry!" Miguel said.

"And some of us are simply rare," Edgar said. "The stuff of legends."

Bill nodded. "I've heard some stories," he said softly. "We lost another Teddycat, Jack, to the humans. We think they were after his claws." He gulped, fighting back a roil of deep unease. His limbs felt light, out of his control. "They probably pulled 'em right out."

"I'm sorry to hear that," Henri said. "And I'm sorry for your loss."

"They want to extract my poison and put it in a dart!" Miguel said.

"I fell asleep," Duffy said, "and when I woke up, I was here."

"Yes, we know the story," said Coco.

"You might want to find a new one," said Edgar, more resigned than cruel.

"There's no escape," Vic hissed. His teeth were frightful, fang-like and too large for his face. "Once the humans have you, you belong to them. They'll lock you in a cage, chop you up, cook you in a stew. They'll cut off your horns, hooves, or tusks and grind 'em into powder."

"That's enough," said Henri, his voice another bolt of lightning. "You know, Vic, at a certain point it just becomes counterproductive."

"I'm simply schooling the boy," Vic said, retreating into the private darkness of his folded wings.

"No, I need to hear this," Bill said. "I need to know everything."

The animals told Bill what little they knew about their location in the jungle. Much of what they said felt fused with the fears they had already listed: The humans were ransacking the jungle, seeking game and gold, hunting and collecting.

"Your man Jack," Henri said. "He's the clue. What the humans did, they'll do to you."

"The humans came into our cave with burning sticks," Vic said. "Many of us choked to death on the smoke, while a few fled out into the light and right into their trap. I am the only one who survived transport. Some, like Henri, believe that I should not tell you these truths. But these truths are all we have."

Henri sighed. "Thank you, Vic."

OTHER THAN THE unknowns of their ultimate fate, every other aspect of this human site seemed to run like clockwork. Food and water was replenished every day, at approximately the same time. Of course the notion of time itself had become a bit slippery, with long stretches of bright, artificial light dulling the animals' instincts and abilities. There was only one window, small and mostly blocked by brush. Only hints of daylight scratched through, and nothing at night.

Some of the animals seemed squarely institutionalized, in thrall to their captors, just as Bill's father had warned. Duffy was a prime example. He was fat and happy, completely at home in his cage. Bill feared that Elena might lean this way. She was young and forgetful, easily influenced and open to suggestion, too young to judge motives or character. After all, she had followed Bill down from Cloud Kingdom. Now he needed her to follow him once more.

At night, the light clicked off without warning. One by one, the animals dropped off into a deep, almost artificial sleep. The room was cold and lonely. Duffy's snores rattled their cages. Bill bid Elena good night, but he could tell she was already dreaming. So he curled up, wondering how Luke, Omar, and Diego were doing. For all he knew the humans had gotten them too, taken them to another site. Or maybe they were still out there, dying of thirst in the middle of the savanna. Or maybe they were leading the humans straight to Cloud Kingdom.

Bill was tired and afraid. His head ached. The mission as first imagined—sneaking into the humans' camp, breaking into and out of multiple cages, busting out Elena without detection—now seemed laughable. The humans had the speed, strength, and motive to demolish Cloud Kingdom in a matter of hours. They could lock every Teddycat in a cage, imprison the entire species, or just ransack the place, plucking claws one by one at their leisure.

He had to warn the others. But first, he needed to escape. Well, before even that he needed a good night's rest. Hopefully his predicament wouldn't seem so dire in the morning. He curled up and tried to sleep.

Chapter

 29

THE LIGHTS SNAPPED on just as suddenly as they had gone out. The brightness burned Bill's eyes. He dug his snout deeper into the crook of his arm, hoping to fall back asleep and wake up someplace else. Duffy was still snoring. There were clicks, flutters, yawns, and yelps as the captives slowly rose to face another day in their cages. But while his first night in the cage had been far from peaceful, Bill did feel more attuned to his surroundings, more aware, and more certain than ever that they needed to escape. He vowed to follow every lead presented. He would not become another caged animal, lapping at his bowl, lost to the wild, instincts fried and wiped. This would not become his new normal. He tried to remember the fear he had felt—in the jungle, on the river, in the savanna—and focus on the thrill of it, the shock and power it delivered. That was what he needed to harness in order to survive. He couldn't let the humans take that away from him.

"When do the humans come with food?" Bill asked.

"Not for a while," Henri said.

"Look at you," Edgar said. "All that big talk last night, and now you want breakfast."

"That's not it," Bill said, though he *was* hungry.

Elena was as bright and chirpy as ever. "Good morning, Bill!" she said, like it was any other day.

"Hi, Elena!" he said, trying to match her enthusiasm.

Just then, the hatch that led to the outside was unsealed and began to draw open with a wheeze.

"Looks like you got your wish," murmured Henri.

The room took on a static stillness as a parade of white-shrouded humans entered. Bill was nearly certain that the human at the front of the line was the one who had captured him, even though he had not gotten a good look at its face or any other identifying characteristics. This certainty grew as the lead human approached his cage and the others formed a small circle.

The next thing he knew, one of them was unlatching his cage. A sliver of opportunity! Bill made himself small, ready to dart. While it was true that he hadn't fully sketched out his escape plan, he *had* promised to chase every chance full throttle. Instead, he surprised and disappointed himself by recoiling as the human stuck its forepaw inside.

The human purred as it reached into the cage.

Bill was in pure reflex mode, frozen somewhere between fight and flight. The human crouched down, and for the first time Bill saw its face: kindly drawn eyes; sharp, freckled cheeks; a wry smile that instantly reminded Bill of his mother's. He was taken aback. This was not the human he had been expecting. He had expected Joe, a tar-streaked smoker, greasy with an evil glint. This human smelled sweet and citrusy. It had straw-colored hairs, which were tucked loosely behind the ears.

The human reached further into the cage and grabbed hold of Bill's left paw. And suddenly, his jungle instincts returned. Or maybe it was just panic, the thought of Jack's torture and the images Vic's stories evoked. Losing a claw would be too great an indignity. He could face failure and capture, but there was no way he was going to live out the rest of his days neu-tered and ashamed. Bill bared his claws and slashed at the human. A jagged ribbon of blood appeared on the human's foreleg, and a small splatter stained the cage. The human yelped and yanked its paw back out. Another human, this one larger and gruffer, approached and slammed the cage shut.

Bill panted as his senses returned. The old panic fizzled into something softer, sadder. He felt guilt and remorse. The circled humans were frantic, clearly fuss-ing over the injured one's wounds and shooting Bill troubled, disapproving looks.

The other animals were silent, on edge. Though contained to their cages, Bill felt them pull away from him. Even Duffy was awake and watchful, his heavy breathing only slightly less labored than his snores. Bill could understand why they would want to create distance between themselves and him, his actions, but he couldn't actually believe that they thought he had done the wrong thing. After all, he hadn't been placed in his cage willingly.

But he could already see that defense wouldn't fly in the eyes of at least one witness: Elena. She looked scared, and not of the humans.

AS SOON AS the humans left in a huff and the exit was once again sealed shut, Bill tried to explain himself to Elena and the others. "I didn't mean to hurt it," he said. "I really didn't. It was self-defense, just a scratch."

"Whatever it was, I hope it was worth it," Henri said. "Rule number one, kid: Don't bite the paw that feeds you."

"It does more than feed," Bill said. "We don't have much time. Who knows what they're doing outside, what they're deciding? We need to break out of here, and fast."

"Bill, just be nice," Elena said.

She was disappointed in him. He knew the feeling all too well. But he would have to make it up to her later. Right now, Bill needed to orchestrate a jailbreak.

There was no telling how the humans would respond to his impulsive violence, and he didn't really want to be around to find out. What if they summoned Joe? He scanned the room for vulnerabilities. There weren't many. Every surface was gleaming, every cage secured. As for cohorts, it seemed unlikely the other animals would be of any assistance. But all was not lost. He still had his claws—for now—and if he could use them to escape his cage, break Elena out (and convince her she was safer with him than with the humans), he might be able to slip out when the humans re-entered. Or maybe the window was the answer. The green forest pressed against the pane. They could crawl out and disappear into the wild. It was definitely big enough for them to fit through, and there was a trickle of rust leaking from one corner.

Bill stared at the window longingly and lapsed into a daydream. He was at home, curled up in his straw and watching the light shift through the clouds. He could hear his mother bustling about and his father working in the garden. He was warm and surrounded by love. All of his friends were nearby. Maia, Luke, Diego, even Omar. Things were simple, back to normal. No, they were better than normal. They were safely situated in a peaceful future where Teddycats and Olingos and other creatures were bound together and stronger than ever. He saw from their faces that he hadn't disappointed them or let them down, hadn't made promises he couldn't keep, hadn't led their family members astray or left them to fend for themselves on a sun-blasted savanna.

Oh, what Bill wouldn't do to see everyone again, happy and free. Until then he would have to survive on dreams. But even Bill was amazed by the vividness and clarity of his fantasy. This sterile room's relentless, buzzing whiteness, its lack of stimuli—all of this must have caused these hallucinations . . .

. . . because there was Maia in the window, so close and so real that Bill felt like he could almost reach out and touch her.

"*Psst,* Bill," said the vision of Maia in the window. "Look alive. We're breaking you out of here."

Chapter

30

IT HAD FINALLY happened. Bill had finally lost it. He was seeing things and hearing voices that weren't really there. He had expected this to happen when he was in the savanna—exhausted, dehydrated, amid blurry waves of heat. But here, in the temperature-controlled lab, the visions were jarring. This didn't bode well for his long-term prospects as a cage dweller.

The vision of Maia was still at the window, appealing to Bill. He turned away to try to shut her off.

"Excuse me, Bill," Henri said.

"Now what?" Bill murmured, trying to sound sane.

"I believe you have a visitor."

Henri unfurled his tail and pointed it to the window.

"Wait. You can see it, too?" Bill asked. His fur stood up, and his heart raced. "Tell me Henri, what exactly do you see?"

Henri slowly craned his neck. Bill's eyes followed his as they landed on the window together. There, Maia smiled impatiently and gave a stiff wave.

"A Teddycat," Henri said. "Female, I believe, with . . ."

Bill flipped. Joy was shooting out of his ears.

"You see what I see! Maia is real!"

"Of course I'm real, you dodo," Maia said. "Now snap out of it! We're bouncing you out."

"How'd you find me?" Bill asked, still reeling.

"I ran into these guys," Maia said.

She turned around, and suddenly, two more faces emerged through the leaves. It was Luke and Diego, snouts pressed against the glass.

"Surprise!" Luke said.

"Good to see you, mate," Diego said. "How they treatin' ya?"

"Fine!" said Bill. "Well, not really. But I'm feeling much better now. And Elena's here!"

"Elena!" Maia cried.

Her sister's head shot up, ears perked.

"Elena!" Maia said again, tapping the glass. "Where are you?"

"Here I am," Elena said. "Down here!"

"There you are!" said Maia, wiping her eyes, their love all but bursting through the wall. "I've come to get you, sweetie."

"How did you find us, anyways?" Bill asked. "No, wait, how did you meet up with Diego and Luke? And where's Omar?"

"We don't have time for a pop quiz," said Maia. "Omar is on lookout, down on the ground. I'll explain the rest later."

The joyful reunion was brief, as everyone remembered the dangers of their situation.

"What's the play, mate?" Diego said. "You got this place all dialed in?"

"I wish," said Bill. "The humans have it wrapped up tight. Do you guys have a plan?"

"Sure we do," Maia said. "First things first, we need a distraction."

Bill was still ecstatic but growing restless. Maia was taking too long to explain the plan. He preferred to be the one dishing them out.

"Food is definitely going to be important if we want to pull this off," said Maia. "But not your food, Bill."

"So then, whose food?"

"The human food."

"The *human* food? They don't bring that in here."

Maia rolled her eyes. "They're setting it up outside right now. It's steaming away under another shelter, mere steps from your cages."

"Mere steps!" said Luke.

"So you're going to sabotage their dinner," Bill said, stroking his chin, "and in the ensuing melee, break us out of here."

"Basically," Maia said. "Does that meet with your approval?"

Bill nodded. "So crazy it just might work."

"Good," said Maia. "Now . . ."

"But there are just a few potential hiccups," Bill said.

Maia groaned.

"In no particular order: How do we guarantee that the one doing the distracting is going to be safe? How do we unseal the human exit? Who's coming with us? Where do we go from here?"

"Do you want to be rescued or not?" said Maia.

"Of course I do," Bill said, "but I don't want to lose anyone else in the process. It's a vicious cycle. You know that."

"You're wasting time and probably scaring Elena," Maia said.

"We just have to do our best," Elena said.

"That's right, sweetie," Maia said, glaring at Bill.

"Can't argue with that," Bill said. "So who's the lure?"

"Well," Maia said, "originally we were going to pull straws, but then . . ."

Omar popped up. "I volunteered."

Chapter

31

ANOTHER WHITE-CLOAKED HUMAN entered the room and refilled water and food. At the first wheeze of the entrance opening, Maia and the others folded back into the green abyss. Bill ate and drank lustily and encouraged the others to as well, especially Elena. They would need their strength, and who knew when they'd have their next meal.

The human stood there for a minute, watching them eat. Could the human tell what was going on just by observing them? Bill couldn't imagine it was any way to read the situation, but still, it was nerve-racking, the way it stood guard, perspiring and breathing heavily in the middle of the room. Finally, the human put its paws under a stream of water that flowed out of a sleek metal contraption by the exit, then left.

Maia and the others reappeared at the window. "Okay, Omar is going to run across the table, cause a scene, and lead the humans on a wild macaw chase." She paused, then turned toward a different set of cages. "Um, no offense."

"None taken," said Coco.

"With all that going on, nobody will hear Diego and me crash through this window. Careful," she said, tapping the surface of the window, "I have a feeling this stuff is going to be sharp when it breaks. Bill, make sure everybody is paying attention."

"Hey, everybody," Bill announced. "Listen up. If you want out, we're making our move. The Teddycat outside is named Maia. She's going to be coming through that window in a few minutes, so watch your heads."

A murmur of excitement whipped through the room. But Bill knew it would be difficult for some of the captive creatures to leave their cages. He needed their trust. "Hey, Henri," said Bill, "can you help me out on this? Be my second-in-command?"

"I'm too old for that, Bill," Henri said. "Thank you for the offer, but I am electing to stay here. I would only slow you down."

"Nonsense," Bill said, "we need you."

"I'm staying put, too," said Edgar the ocelot. "I'd hate to get caught up and land you all in trouble."

"That's just dead wrong, Edgar," Bill said. "You're, like, the fastest thing in the jungle."

"It's been too long," said Edgar, as Henri sighed in agreement.

Bill stood on his hind legs and gripped the front of his cage. "All right, everybody, listen up. Maia—Elena's sister and my friend—has been nice enough to come down here and draw up an escape plan. Now, you are all invited to come along, but I need to know before we get started and things start to unfold. So, a show of paws, claws, wings . . . whatever."

They went around the room. Thankfully, Elena was on board. Duffy was noncommittal. Miguel and Coco were ecstatic. Vic said he thought they were all doomed but hey, why not? Edgar said he was in only if Henri was in. Still, Henri demurred.

"Come on," Bill said. "Just think about all the life you've got left to live out there."

"I suppose it would be nice to feel useful again," Henri said, his tail swinging.

"Yes!" said Bill. "Let's put that tail back to work."

They heard the clatter of the human dinner before anything else. Funny-looking tools and vessels made of metal went flying upward in sudden confusion as the white sheet—gripped between Omar's teeth—disappeared beneath the altar upon which they dined.

The volume rose even higher as the humans' shock turned to bedlam. They were hollering, running in circles, chasing after Omar. The flimsy wooden things they propped their backsides on tipped backward. Hot, greasy water spilled from a sizzling contraption and splashed over everything.

It was the perfect cover: The window broke easily, and the shards—which were just as sharp as Maia had predicted—fell safely to the floor.

Maia and Diego slipped down into the room and immediately went to Bill's cage.

"No," he protested, "get Elena first. That's why you're here. Don't worry about me."

"You free the older ones first," Maia said. "Many paws, light work."

"I never thought of it that way," Bill said.

"It's one of those seemingly selfish but secretly smart moves," said Maia, as she unlatched his cage. "Kind of your specialty, Bill."

Bill was free in seconds, and the three of them got to work uncaging the others. Maia scooped up Elena, and the two of them spun in circles of happy relief. Bill unlocked Henri's cage, and for the first time they stood face-to-face. "Nice to formally meet you," said Bill.

"The pleasure is all mine," said Henri, promptly turning to free Edgar and Coco.

Maia freed Miguel, which just left Diego and Vic, who were engaged in some kind of standoff. "Let's go, guys," said Bill, as he rooted around the room, looking for extra food to bindle up and take with them. "Grab Vic and we're out of here."

"Little guy gives me the creeps, mate," Diego said.

"Right back at you," Vic hissed.

Bill found the feed sack and tossed it to Henri, who clasped it with his tail. "After everything we've been through, Diego, this is where you draw the line?"

"He's upside-down," Diego said, shuddering. "Makes my fur crawl."

"Vic is a friend, and you need friends to survive in the jungle," Bill said. "You know that."

"Oh, all right," Diego said, swiping at the latch. "Come on out, ya little bugger."

THE SUDDEN BURST into freedom delivered quite a shock to the captives. With the exception of Elena, who was in Maia's arms, they were woozy, still finding their bearings. Meanwhile, Omar continued to cause commotion. The window, while large enough for everyone to fit through, was awkwardly sized, and was now rimmed with sharp shards that clung stubbornly to the sides. Those who were not natural climbers (all except Maia, Diego, Henri, and Bill) or who couldn't fly (like Vic and Coco could) would have to go slowly to avoid getting sliced and snagged on the shards.

Maia and Elena went through first. Vic and Coco flew out, with Miguel catching a ride on Coco's back. One by one they disappeared into the leaves, safely out of sight.

This left Diego and Bill with Duffy, Edgar, and Henri. Henri was an able climber in his younger, wild days, but such a long time in a cage had taken its toll.

"We're going to help each other get out of here," Bill said. "Don't worry, we won't leave without anyone."

A shrill call—like nothing Bill had ever heard come out of any animal or human—rang out from somewhere in the camp.

"That can't be good," Diego said.

"Better hurry," Bill said.

They pushed cages against the wall and helped Duffy up to the window. His unwieldy body rolled over the ledge. He was jiggly and ticklish, a bad combination.

"Grab hold of the branches, Duffy," said Bill. "Grab hold and pull yourself out."

Instead, the sloth grabbed a cluster of leaves and ate it, closing his eyes, smiling dreamily.

"Don't you dare fall asleep, Duff!" Henri said.

Edgar whimpered anxiously.

Outside, the commotion seemed to be settling down some. It wouldn't be long before the humans took stock of the situation and decided to check on the captives.

One lesson Bill had learned on this mission: It usually didn't do any good to holler at a slowpoke. That just rattled them. But it wasn't every day that Bill shepherded a multispecies exodus from a human fortress, so he figured this might be an exception to the rule and gave it a shot.

"Get a move on, Duffy!" he shouted. "I'm not going down because you fell asleep halfway through an escape!"

Henri dropped the food he was holding—still secure in its human-made pouch—and balanced himself against the wall. His tail rose up behind him and curled around Duffy's slumping midsection. The sloth's snores turned high-pitched as the graying fur around Henri's eyes narrowed to a brilliant fold of white.

With gasps and grunts Henri used his tail to lift the sloth over the ledge and into the trees.

"Well, that couldn't have gone worse," Edgar said.

"Good news," Bill said. "You're up next."

"Bad news," Edgar said. "I'm afraid of heights."

"No, you are not," Bill said.

"I'm afraid it's true," Henri said.

The alien-sounding shriek was still bleating. The humans' distraction would soon be over and it wouldn't be long before they closed in on the source of the mischief. They had limited time.

"Look," Bill said. "I've lived my life high up in the trees. I can climb higher than you can imagine. You know what I say? All you have to do is get in the swing. Find the rhythm of the jungle and you'll be walking on air in no time."

"Ah, you see . . . I belong on the ground," Edgar said. "It's my nerves."

"Sometimes we have to adapt," Bill said. "It's painful . . ."

"But necessary," said Henri, as his tail snaked around Edgar's sleek thorax, squeezed, and tossed him out the window.

"Nice!" Bill said. He jumped up onto the cage, skittered up the wall, and leaned out the window. "Edgar, you okay?"

There was only a rustle; all else was drowned out by the constant shrieking, the humans, the panic.

"Hey, Edgar?" he said again. "You make it?"

"Henri needs to work on his manners," Edgar said, safely tangled in the brush.

"Quick and painless," Bill said. "What could be better?"

Bill and Henri were the only remaining captives. The old monkey was a tad larger than Bill had predicted, but he had proved to be an invaluable part of the escape. It was on Bill to make good on his promises. He felt the burden of leadership settle on his shoulders.

No, wait. That burden was just Henri, preparing to vault the window by climbing up Bill's body.

"Steady," Henri murmured.

"Right back at you," said Bill.

Henri's opposable thumbs were no doubt very helpful in the wild, but at that moment they were really digging into Bill's neck.

"Somehow I've . . ." Henri huffed.

"How did you get spun around like that?" asked Bill.

"I've absolutely no idea," Henri said. "But now I'm stuck."

Bill ground his paws into the floor and tried to push Henri out by the legs. It was no use. His backside was out the window while his limbs still dangled in the lab. Bill and the monkey met eyes—Henri wore a pained expression. He was embarrassed and afraid. Bill was trying to brainstorm what to do next, when he heard a familiar sound.

The big hatch wheezed open again, and a disheveled human entered. Bill and Henri froze. The human was only steps away, kicking mud off its feet. The white shroud was soiled, streaked with food and grass stains. It seemed Omar had really caused a ruckus. He'd performed a truly heroic feat. Bill felt happy for his friend, and proud, as he pushed and pushed the spider monkey.

But Henri wouldn't budge.

The human was standing before the mounted water fountain, wetting small fibrous scraps and dabbing them on the stains. Miraculously, it still hadn't noticed the commotion by the window.

"Use your tail," Bill pleaded.

"I'm trying," Henri said. "There's nothing out there!"

"We're here!" Maia said from the other side. "Grab on to us!"

"That's Maia," Bill said. "She'll pull you out."

"Ow!" said Henri, but finally his body began to move.

The human kept fussing with his stained garments. He was like a cat, licking himself in the corner. It seemed unlikely that such a fastidious creature would survive in the jungle, but Bill could only be thankful for each blessed additional second.

"Hurry!" Bill said. "We've got zero time!"

"Oooh," groaned Henri. "This is most unpleasant. I told you this was going to happen! Through a window. Absurd! I haven't been able to fit through a window since . . ."

"You can . . . do . . . it," Bill said, pushing with every fiber he had, his muscles clenched and sore, his claws digging into the ground. "Maia, pull!"

"We're trying!" Maia said.

"He's a big boy, mate," Diego grunted.

All at once, Henri slipped through the window frame with an audible *pop!*

The human looked up.

The white shroud was wet, and the hides tied to its feet had been kicked off. Bill locked eyes with the human. He felt the cold stare bore through him. There was a lot he wanted to say to it. He wanted to explain the pain the humans had caused, chastise the arrogance of snatching a child in a cage and taking her away. He wanted to make them feel the loss of Felix, the strife in Cloud Kingdom. But there wasn't time, and the human wouldn't have understood.

Instead Bill climbed up the wall and vaulted out the window, back into the brush. The human just stood there, dumbfounded and helpless.

BILL QUICKLY REACHED the others, who were huddled in a small clearing, stretching their uncaged muscles and checking one another for scrapes and other injuries. Vic and Coco were perched on a crooked branch. Henri and Edgar were lumped in the corner, overcome with emotion. Luke and Miguel were fast friends, slapping fives. And there was Maia, cradling Elena, sweet relief streaming from her eyes.

"Everybody good?" Bill asked.

"Amazingly, yes. I think so," Maia said.

"We're going home, Bill," Elena said.

"Now that's what I'm talking about, Elena!" said Bill. "But where were you hiding that fighting spirit back in the lab?"

"She was just playing it cool," Maia said. "Weren't you, girlie?"

"Yeah," Elena said, giggling.

The shrill shriek was still blaring. Blinking, roaring human machines were coming to life. Black clouds billowed out of steel tubes. There were shouts and slamming, and an ominous whirring as a strong wind kicked up and blew the brush sideways. Soon their escape route would be flattened, overrun.

"Let's get outta here," said Diego.

"Right behind you," said Edgar.

"Wait a minute," said Bill, "where's Omar?"

"We're not sure," Maia said.

"We can't leave without him!" said Bill.

"He volunteered . . ." Maia said. "For a job he knew was dangerous."

"Yeah, for the most dangerous job," Bill said. "We wouldn't have made it out if it weren't for him."

"He knows the rendezvous point," said Maia. "And the backup rendezvous. He'll be there. He'll be fine."

"What if he's not?" Bill said. "What if these humans call for Joe? He's still out there!"

"We have to leave now, Bill."

"Not without Omar!"

"We gotta go, mate," Diego said.

"There are others involved, Bill," said Maia. "You don't know the whole story. Don't blow this escape now, not when we're so close. Please, just trust me."

Bill bit his lip. The chaotic sounds surrounding them were completely foreign, but he knew that the news of their escape was spreading throughout the site. The humans were mobilizing. It didn't feel right to leave Omar behind, but Maia was right: It wasn't his plan. His mind swirled. It seemed like no matter where he was or who he was with, doing the right thing—if the right thing could even be identified—was never easy.

Bill sighed. Omar was a brave Teddycat. Maia and the others had gotten them this far. He would have to trust his friends to carry them home.

The wind picked up, loud and pressing as it chopped the shriek into a mournful wail.

"Okay," Bill said. "Let's go."

Chapter

THE FUGITIVES HUSTLED through the wilderness, away from the camp. Bill felt his instincts slowly returning. The air was warm and fragrant, filled with the buzz and stench of the jungle. He shook his head in disbelief. Teddycats were not meant to be locked up in cages! Oh, well, the humans had been forced to learn that lesson the hard way.

Bill was impressed with Maia's skills. She moved with the grace and purpose of a warrior, all while carrying Elena. The others were doing their best to keep up. Old Diego was tough as ever, limping out front, a natural scout. And Bill was impressed by the captive animals, too. Edgar had taken his words to heart—he really could be the fastest thing around—and Henri had successfully shaken off the trauma of fitting through the window. The group moved with a desperate cohesiveness down the narrow path.

Suddenly, Bill was struck by something Maia had said back there. *There were others.* Who was she talking about? Where were they now?

The sounds of the humans receded as they drove deeper into the jungle, but some of the weaker trees still shook from the wind, and the sharp smell of their smoke still lingered.

"I hate to ask this," Henri said between pants, "but how much farther are we going?"

"Not long now," Luke said.

"Just keep low and stay moving," said Maia.

"Yeah, what she said," said Bill.

The path grew more treacherous, etched as it was into the face of a guano-streaked rock face. They began a heady, scrambling ascent, until the trail dead-ended at a spooky clearing.

"Now where?" Bill asked.

"Quick, in here," Maia said, pointing into the darkness. Bill squinted. It was a large cave, pitch-black and dripping with condensation.

"No way," Edgar said.

"Suit yourself," said Maia.

"Looks just dandy to me," Vic said.

"Exactly my point," Edgar said.

Bill wasn't too excited about the cave either, but he didn't want to appear ungrateful or intimidated.

"I'll stand watch," said Coco, spreading her wings.

"Me too," said Bill, puffing his chest and crossing his arms.

"Bill," Maia said, "don't be a clown. Get in here."

"Fine," said Bill.

Somehow, the inside of the cave was even darker than Bill could have imagined. Every drip echoed endlessly as they slunk deeper and deeper into the abyss. Then, suddenly, there was light. A torch. He blinked furiously as the flames soared and settled. Huddled there before him was a large group of Teddycats.

"Bill!" It was a voice Bill would recognize anywhere.

"Mom!"

Marisol rushed out of the darkness and threw her arms around her son. Bill was overwhelmed with love, relief, and confusion.

"Mom, what are you doing here?"

Marisol pulled back. Her eyes were filled with tears. She choked back a sob, then squeezed her son again.

"What happened?" Bill asked.

He figured the longer she went without answering, the worse it had to be. His heart sank as the silence stretched and deepened. The Teddycats looked down, averted their eyes. Their faces were drawn tight with sorrow. There were Elders, Teddycats from all over the Kingdom. And there was Omar!

"Omar! Buddy! You made it!" Bill said, forgetting himself and the situation for a moment.

"Hey, Bill," said Omar, but his spirits were clearly just as low as those of the others.

"Mom, what happened? How did you guys find us?"

Marisol was still shaking. She clutched him so close Bill could barely breathe.

"Somebody tell me what's going on!"

Luke stepped forward. "After the human captured you in the savannah, we started tracking you right away. We followed you and the human back to the jungle. We were just a few hours behind you, following a fresh trail, when we met up with Maia and your mom and the others. They were . . ."

Luke mumbled something and slipped back into the darkness.

"They were . . . what?" said Bill. "*Then* what happened? Why won't somebody just tell me? I can't help until I know what's going on!"

The Teddycats whimpered.

"You were right," Maia said, stepping into the light. "You were right about Cloud Kingdom, Bill. We can't go back there. Right after you left, the humans attacked. They knew exactly where we were, and they knew exactly what they wanted. They went on a rampage. They . . . they took the claws, and the lives, of so many. We've lost brothers and sisters, mothers and fathers, friends and family. We're the only ones left, Bill. We're the only ones who made it out alive."

Many of the Teddycats were weeping. The flame cast darting shadows on the walls. Bill felt like he was in a nightmare: friends from all walks of life, together in an unfamiliar place, hiding from danger. He was woozy. For a moment, he missed his cage.

Bill scanned the cave for his father, but he wasn't there. A cold lump grew in his throat. He swallowed it down, straight to his heart, and forced himself to hope that Big Bill, the strongest Teddycat he ever knew, had somehow made it out of this alive.

"That's not all," said Luke. "When we ran into Maia and the others, we shared our stories and learned a few things. The humans who attacked Cloud Kingdom aren't the same ones who took you and Elena."

Bill turned away, remembering Felix's theory about

the two kinds of humans. So Joe got Jack and Luke, and he and Elena had been snatched up by the others. The smoky fire, the ugly debris, the swapped signals—it was all starting to make sense. They had been chasing two different villains. No wonder it had felt as if the humans were everywhere.

"Either way, we need a new place to live," Maia said. "And we were hoping you might have some ideas."

Bill was doubled over, raw anger burning in his stomach. He needed vengeance. He needed to lash back at the humans, all the humans, his claws gleaming and slicing as he took back his home and made them pay for the pain they caused. Bill didn't care which humans got in his way. He wouldn't rest until they were forced to account for their crimes. The humans wanted claws, Bill would give them claws. He growled. His mother tried to comfort him. He twisted away. But then he saw the Teddycats, wounded and terrified. Somebody had to take care of them. Somebody had to lead the way. Bill thought back to what Felix had said.

If you get lost, just look to the horizon, the last line of light.

He straightened up, swallowing the pain and anger. "I know where we need to go."

Bill couldn't say much more. It was only a feeling, an instinct, an orientation, something he felt tugging on his heart, like a guiding star. Luckily, the other Teddycats were desperate for guidance. Nobody asked too many questions, which was all for the best, as they would need to preserve their energy for the journey ahead. They divided what little food there was and vowed to embark at dawn.

Chapter

OUTSIDE THE CAVE, the jungle awoke, yawning to life with the flap and chatter of a new day. Bill had barely slept. Instead, he spent the night trying to appear calm and confident. Of course, inside he was a mess. What if Felix's words failed them? He wasn't even sure what they meant. And what if he led the Teddycats right back into the path of the humans? Well, maybe that was just life in the jungle. They would all have to get used to it.

Bill and Elena bid farewell to Henri, Edgar, Miguel, Coco, and Vic. They were sad to splinter off, but they had their own destinies to discover.

"Good luck to you, Bill Garra," Henri said. "You have managed to teach an old monkey a few new tricks.

I wouldn't have bet on you that first day we met inside, but I'll never forget our time together."

"Don't sell yourself short, Henri," Bill said. "You were the real rabble-rouser in there. I was just following your lead."

Edgar was noticeably anxious about re-entering the wild. He pulled Bill aside. "You really think I'll be all right out there?"

"You'll be fine," Bill said. "Just be true to yourself."

"Easy for you to say," Edgar said.

"Oh, please," said Bill. "I'm as lost as anyone."

"These Teddycats will follow you anywhere," said Edgar solemnly. "Take care of them."

"I will," Bill said. "Hey, Edgar, don't forget how fast you can go."

Edgar rolled his eyes but smiled as he slipped into the brush.

"Miguel, stay safe," said Bill. "I'd hate to get shot by a Miguel-laced dart any time soon."

"You got it, Bill," Miguel said, his translucent skin blushing slightly.

"Coco, Vic, behave yourselves."

"Get going already," said Vic.

"Seriously," Coco said.

Diego, keeping watch by the cave mouth, called down to the others. It was time to start off. The journey would only grow more dangerous the longer they waited.

The Teddycats began to inch their way out of the darkness. They were streaked with mud, cut, and bruised. But there was a determination in their eyes. Bill recognized it immediately. It was the same look he had seen in Omar and Diego when they set off across the savannah, the look Luke had when his mother clutched him to her chest, the look Elena gave him when he had misbehaved in the lab. The Teddycats and their allies were stronger than they knew.

Bill hoped the same held true for him.

FELIX HAD SAID to follow the light, so Bill headed first for high ground, then west, following the blazing arc of the sun. Behind him Luke and Diego led the charge. Omar and Maia brought up the rear, gently encouraging stragglers. In the middle was a struggling mass of Teddycats, bedraggled and spent, grief rising off them like steam.

"Where are we going, Bill?" Luke asked. "You can tell me."

"I wish I could," Bill said. "That's the truth. Only, I'll know it when I see it."

"You Teddycats," Luke said. "So secretive."

"We're bein' hunted by humans, mate," Diego said. "Let's hope we can keep a few things close to the chest."

Bill decided that it wasn't the right moment to remind Diego of the Teddycats' future as jungle citizens. After all, the scout had already proven himself courageous, tolerant, and inexhaustible many times over. Bill couldn't believe there could possibly be an arrangement that Diego could not handle or learn to accept.

"What do I tell the others if they ask where we're going?" Luke persisted.

"Why would they ask you?" Diego said.

"I'm approachable," Luke said.

"Well, you definitely have a way of getting underfoot," said Bill. "I'll give you that. Anyone asks, we're headed west."

"West," Luke repeated, with a hushed reverence.

"You *do* realize this will lead us back to the river," Diego said.

"It's looking that way," Bill said. "We'll make it across."

"Remember last time?" Diego said.

"At least we'll get a drink," said Bill. He was bleary with fatigue, hunger, and thirst. A dunk in the river didn't sound so bad. This time he would just stay away from supercharged eels and sudden hundred-foot drops.

"What happened last time?"

It was Marisol, pushing up from the middle.

"Hi, Mom," said Bill. "How's everybody doing back there?"

"Oh, they're doing their best, poor dears," Marisol said.

"I'll bet they're wondering where we're going," Luke said.

Bill shot him a glare.

"You know what?" Marisol replied. "I think we're just happy for a second chance. For too long we hid away in Cloud Kingdom, and look what that brought us."

"How's . . ." Bill started, then trailed off and tried again. "Where's Dad?"

Marisol sighed, sadness falling upon her face. "Your father is safe, in hiding with some of the Elders, but he decided to stay behind in Cloud Kingdom to learn more about the humans. I begged him to come with us, but in the end he did what he thought was best."

"I guess I understand that," said Bill, a pang in his chest. "I've learned that the right thing doesn't always look the same to everybody."

"You're so grown up, Bill," Marisol said, rubbing her son's neck.

"Hey," said Luke, "that's what *my* mom said about him, too."

"Are you sure Dad's safe?" Bill asked. In his mind he had an image of his father hiding in the brush as the humans ransacked the Kingdom. "Once the humans know where you are . . . well, it's hard to find a hiding spot that's safe from them."

"Your father is a very smart and brave Teddycat," said Marisol. "He knows what he's doing. We have to trust him. And he made me promise to tell you that he loves you very much, and that he's proud of everything you've done."

"He really said that?" Bill asked.

"Of course!" Marisol said. "Did you really think he ever felt any other way? Sure, he's a grump—don't even get me started—but he's not a total jerk."

Bill nodded, his eyes filling with tears. It felt like

the whole of his heart was finally clicking into place, like a puzzle. "I guess sometimes it was just hard to tell."

"Fathers don't like to look vulnerable," Marisol said. "And I don't think your grandfather was much of a cuddler. But I'll bet the next time we see Big Bill, he'll make it clear enough."

BILL MARCHED FORWARD with renewed vigor, growing more sure of his direction with each step. He wished Felix were there to see him; he wished Felix had heard what his mother said, but maybe Felix had suspected as much all along.

They were deep in unfamiliar forest. An eerie calm descended. There were only umbrella trees, stark and skinny until their wide crowns bloomed and mingled. An arched canopy blocked most light. Bill's first impulse was to rush through the shadowy gauntlet. Instead, he slowed their pace, allowing the group room to breathe.

He remembered the sensation of being watched out on the savanna. He felt a similar sensation creeping up his neck. Halfway through the dark passage, just as the easy strides were beginning to wear on him, he felt a bolt of recognition.

"Freeze!" he said, rearing up and throwing back his arms.

The company froze.

"What do you see?" Diego asked.

Before them was just flat ground, a scattering of mulchy undergrowth.

"Loan me your walking stick," Bill said.

Reluctantly, Diego handed over the handsome shard of bone. Bill held it overhead and brought it down, whacking a seemingly benign patch of ground. Just like that, a swath of netting snapped into a teardrop shape and then shot up into the canopy. The trap hung above them, slack and empty except for the walking stick.

"Good eye, Bill!" said Luke, looking at the trap with frightened recognition. "But any word on where we're going?"

"That was *my* blasted stick," Diego mumbled.

"I owe you one," Bill said.

"Good ones are rare," said Diego.

"That's what makes them valuable," Bill said.

THE ROAR OF the river sent ripples of panic through the ranks of Teddycats. The water had always served as a natural barrier, and in their state they were all quick to fall back on this line.

Maia nudged Bill. "Say something," she whispered, as the Teddycats inched away from the jagged banks and began to fret and panic.

Bill wondered how many convincing words it was going to take to lead them to wherever they were going. He tried to remember all the low points in his life, and what he wished somebody would have told him then. The words of Felix and Big Bill came first to his mind.

"I know it feels strange and unnatural," said Bill. "But we need to cross this river in order to be free. Remember, we have done this before. We have survived far worse. Here's the plan."

THE TEDDYCATS BROKE out into groups and hacked away at the skinny trees.

"These trees are too tall," croaked Ramon, the Elder. He was gray and weak. Bill was surprised he had survived the human attack. "We should *climb* these trees instead."

There were murmurs of agreement.

"Yes, we should climb these trees," Ramon said, rediscovering the authoritative tone he belted from his perch in the Fountain for all those years, "and build a new home in the clouds!"

This proclamation was met with some hollow cheers.

"That's not the way forward!" Bill said. "Together we can fell these trees and use them to cross the river. If we choose to hide in the trees, we may be safe tonight, but not for long."

As if on cue, a huge tree came crashing down.

Diego hopped onto the trunk. "Get to fellin'," he told the others, blowing wood dust from his claw. He snapped a branch and leaned against it for a moment, weighing it in his paw, then whipped some saplings and jabbed at some invisible foes. "This'll do."

By dusk they had a working bridge.

"Nice job," Maia said. "Clearly you've done this before."

"We still need to get everyone on the same page," said Bill. "And then across."

He was watching Ramon out of the corner of his eye. The Elder was holding court with a huddle of other Cloud Kingdom notables, their whispering punctuated with furtive gestures.

"Don't worry about them," Maia said. "They're skittish, but they'll do it."

"It's a good thing they weren't around last time," Luke said.

Bill rolled his eyes. "Will everyone stop talking about last time?"

"What happened last time?" asked Maia.

"He won't say," Marisol whispered.

"I got shocked by an eel and we went over a waterfall, okay? Any other questions? We still have to cross this river, and we have to do it before nightfall."

"Now *that's* leadership," Marisol said, then poked Bill in the tummy. "Zap!"

"Just tell us the truth, Bill," Maia said. "We can handle it. You've been through a lot. Guess what? So have we."

"I know," said Bill. "I'm sorry."

Maia took Bill's paw and squeezed it.

Chapter

BILL CROSSED THE bridge first to demonstrate its stability. He scurried across easily. "Just don't look down!" he called back, knowing it was unlikely anyone would follow that advice.

If it had been completely up to him, the logs would have been dropped in another location, someplace with a slackening current, a stable bank on both sides, and far fewer rocks. But it was out of his control. As they well knew, the river was wild and unpredictable. There was no way to tell if a klick up or down would be any better, and they didn't have scouts to send out.

It had been Luke's idea to carve notches into the top logs to improve grip as well as mark the distance.

Bill hadn't really noticed them during his crossing, but he had no doubt that they would be appreciated by less-experienced woodsmen.

He tried to stay calm and positive as he watched the first group, led by Omar, notch by notch. The group comprised mostly Elders, who moved slowly and deliberately, lashed together paw to paw. The sun was beginning to set. Feelings of urgency rushed through Bill, and he tried his hardest to calm himself down. One by one the worn and wrinkled Elders reached the opposite bank. Many cried tears of relief when they reached the other side.

"Okay," Bill said, allowing himself a smile, "send the next group over."

The middle rank was led by a determined Marisol. Her eyes were clear, her paws set. "Let's move!" she shouted. Her charges crossed easily. Bill began to relax. They were almost there. He could feel it. Back on land, his mother embraced him.

Maia led the final passing. She had Elena on her shoulders. It was obvious that she had no plans of letting go of her sister, no matter what.

They were halfway across the river when a log began to wobble.

"Keep going!" Bill said.

The worst thing they could do was stop, but of course that's what many chose to do. Lucky for Bill, his impulse was to always keep moving.

"You have to keep going!" Bill urged. "If you quit now, more of us will be at risk."

Maia pushed forward, Elena gripping her neck tighter than ever. But the Teddycats behind her had lost their confidence. They stepped too heavily and jostled one another.

"Use your claws!" said Maia, but panic had already seized them. The other logs began to shift, then one began to roll.

"Maia, run!" Bill shouted.

Every second the Teddycats held back made their situation that much more dire. This panic loop drove some to paralysis, others to mania. They began to climb over one another, trying to reach steady ground. As the first log began to separate from the others, a few fell through and down to the water. Each splash was a spear that lanced through the crowd.

Maia and Elena were still ahead, struggling to maintain momentum on the listing log. They were close enough to the bank for Bill to see the terror in their eyes. He fought the urge to rush out and meet them. As badly as he wanted to, he knew it would only create more commotion. But suddenly, Maia slipped and fell by the wayside. As she fell, she lunged her arms forward, claws facing out. One dug into the wood. She kicked and squirmed, suspended over the rushing water.

The force of the fall had jostled Elena down her sister's back. She was holding on to Maia's tail. The water was mere feet below her, black and endless. The Teddycats howled powerless cries as the two dangled. Those still crossing froze in place, while those already on solid ground turned to Bill. He felt sick, helpless. This could not be the way the mission ended. He got down on his belly and inched over the bank. Rocks, leaves, and clods of mud tumbled down to the water, the resulting ripples swallowed up by the fast-moving current.

"Don't panic," Bill shouted, as calmly as possible. His fur shot straight up. He felt like he had been zapped by that eel all over again. "Maia, can you reach up with your other paw?"

"I'll try," Maia said, her voice strangled with fear and exertion. She raised her other arm but could only graze the wood. Elena slipped further down her tail.

"Maia, help!" Elena cried.

A few of the Teddycats who had already fallen were working their way to the shore. Others on the bank found some relief in this, until a dark form began to slice the surface of the water. Bill felt a chill of recognition. It was a crocodile, the big one Diego had sworn he'd seen.

Twenty feet long, scales like boulders, teeth like knives.

"Boris," Diego whispered, his eyes wide, then narrowed, with fear.

"Don't look down," Bill said.

"What?" Maia cried. "What is it?"

Boris circled the area beneath them. His thick yellow stripe cut through the surface. Elena was an easy leap away, and Maia would likely be pulled down with her. The Teddycats' terror grew in volume and fervor. Those still on the log rushed forward, as if chased.

The log rolled as they scrambled, dropping Maia closer to the water. Elena dipped, and the Teddycats gasped.

"Just hold on!" Bill cried.

Boris tightened his circle. He was so large he seemed to create his own current. His length was shockingly immense, as long as the log. The Teddycats could have raced across *his* back. Slowly his tail began to move side to side in a gradually building thrash. Maia tried to pull herself up as Elena clutched her flailing limbs.

"Maia, you have to climb," Bill said. "Please. You've done it a million times before."

Maia growled and tried again to stick her other claw into the log, but it was rolling down the sloping bank. Boris's mass seemed to swell. He was the entire river, as invincible as the water itself.

Elena looked down and shrieked.

The scream sharpened Maia's resolve, as well as Boris's appetite. His tail quickened as it gathered strength. Bill couldn't watch. He was about to throw his paws over his eyes when he felt a familiar one on his shoulder.

"Go to them," Marisol said. She was on her belly too, right next to him. "It's okay to risk everything for the ones you love. But you already know that."

Bill leapt up. "Thanks, Mom."

He quickly climbed an umbrella tree to the very top. Behind him, the sun was setting. All the colors were draining, disappearing. He needed the light so he would know where to go, but he would have to trust his instincts.

The canopy was a tangle of vines. Bill got to work on the knots and snarls. Maia's cries drifted up to him, distant and desperate. Gradually the vine grew longer and longer. Just as the cries reached a new, terrible pitch he closed his eyes and jumped.

The log was really rolling as Bill dropped down. The vine almost reached Maia, but not quite. He gripped the frayed end with a paw and stretched his body as long as it would go.

"Maia, grab hold of my paw!"

"I can't reach!" said Maia.

Boris's head emerged. The eyes on the side were a ghastly yellow, glowing in the dark water. Slowly, his jaw began to open. Slivers of shockingly white fangs, then an endless row. The jaw appeared to unhinge, opening wider and wider. Elena's cries echoed down through the valley.

Bill strained until he thought his arm would fall off.

"Maia, grab my paw! You can do it!"

Maia narrowed her eyes, took a breath, and lunged.

Chapter

35

"**T**HAT WAS A close one," Bill said.

"I thought we agreed to never talk about it again," Maia said.

The sky was slowly ceding to purple. Fireflies were out in full force, as numerous as stars. The Teddycats were in a daze, trudging forward as the last sliver of sun rested just above the trees. Bill's heart skidded. He didn't know where to go. The tug of Felix's words had led him to this point, and now the light had met the horizon. Soon the darkness would be no more reassuring than it had been in the cave. They were facing another steep hill, more barely penetrable brush.

Doubt clouded Bill's resolve. Maybe the Teddycats weren't built for the jungle; maybe their home would always be temporary, a makeshift respite in the trees or whatever wisp of safety they could find. How many dangers could Bill lead his friends and family through before they gave up hope?

They were doomed to spend yet another night in an unwelcoming section of the wild, and another day chasing some semblance of home.

"I'm sorry," Bill said.

"For what?" Maia asked.

As with everything else lately, Bill wasn't exactly sure.

"You'll know it when you see it," said Maia, understanding Bill's silence.

"Let's try for the top of this hill," Bill said. "We'll feel better at a higher elevation."

They hacked through the brush. Bill ripped it down with desperate strokes of his claws. His hopes dimmed with the sky. There was only an etching of daylight remaining, thin as a vein. But as they reached the crest of the hill, a crack appeared, like a keyhole in the darkness. The crest split right down the middle, with what looked like just enough room for the Teddycats to squeeze through.

It was the ravine! The final line of light!

A lump formed in Bill's gut and worked its way up to his throat. Their promised refuge had finally appeared. He waited as the Teddycats caught up and gathered around him. As they assembled, they gasped with deep recognition. Bill felt as if he were watching himself from some remove as he slipped down and wedged his way between the narrow sides. Diego, Luke, Maia, Elena, and Omar followed, the rock faces nearly pinching them as they sucked in their bellies and pushed forward. Gradually the ravine began to widen, and the horizon reappeared. All of the colors seemed to pool before them in a peaceful basin, stretching forward to illuminate a sparkling vista.

Bill felt a stab of recognition. The sense of remove evaporated, and he crashed back into himself with relief.

"This is it," said Bill. "This is our home. This is Horizon Cove."

The Teddycats scurried out of the ravine and immediately began to frolic in the thick, colorful grasses. They rolled in the rich mud and nibbled on the silky, fragrant flowers, luminous fungi, and a breathtaking abundance of sweetmoss. Frogs sang as the fireflies popped.

"This is the life," Diego said. Tears filled his good eye. "I wish Jack could see this."

"You did it, Bill!" Luke said.

"This isn't just for us Teddycats," said Bill. "We're jungle citizens now. I personally deputize you to run back to the Olingo den and bring them here."

"Yes!" Luke said. "Wait, right now?"

Bill laughed. "Whenever you're ready, bud."

Luke watched the gleeful celebration erupt around them. "I could use a night off, I think."

"I think we all could," Bill said.

Maia and Elena were with their parents, playing in the ferns. An elated Marisol joined Luke and Bill as they took in the joyful scene.

"I'm proud of you, Bill," said Marisol, kissing his cheeks and forehead. "We *all* are."

"A part of me thought I'd never see you again," Bill admitted, as all the emotions that had built up during their wild journey—the ups and downs, doubts and fears, losses and dangers, friends and foes—swelled in his chest. There might be no seasons in the jungle, but Bill still felt a shift in the air.

"Makes it all the sweeter, doesn't it?" said Marisol. She continued pecking his face and head, and he wasn't the slightest bit embarrassed.

The Teddycats passed the night rejoicing, exploring the cove, and honoring those they had lost. With a renewed sense of hope, they spoke of the return of a lost feeling, a sensation of immersion, of souls at rest. Even the Elders joined the celebration. Bill fleetingly wondered if he would get an apology from Ramon, but there was plenty of time for that. The important thing was that they had made it. They were safe. There would be no shortage of challenges in the future, as they learned to coexist in the chaos.

IT WAS NEARLY dawn when they began to settle. Bill and Luke were curled up, drowsily discussing their good fortune, chuckling over missteps and wrong turns, when a fierce howl cut through the jungle.

The Teddycats froze. A collective chill ran through them all. Suddenly, there were eyes all around them, glowing and vicious.

"Bill, what's happening?" Luke whispered.

"I don't know," Bill said.

Shapes began to emerge from the darkness. Bill started to make out certain features: wide, jagged shoulders. Snarling snouts. Eyes bright yellow with hate. The Teddycats shrunk into a huddle as the predators advanced.

Bill found Marisol. "Mom, what are these? What's happening?"

"I don't know," said Marisol, her voice laced with terror.

Maia squeezed between them. "What do we do?"

Bill bared his claws. They glinted in the rising sun as the shapes continued to creep forward.

"This is our home," Bill said. "We fight for it."

THE END

TURN THE PAGE FOR A SNEAK PEEK OF THE NEXT

ADVENTURE!

Chapter

1

BILL GARRA HELD the line as the glowing, green eyes of the shapeless intruders crept closer, gathering into sinister clusters. The Teddycats were locked together, prepared to defend Horizon Cove, their newfound sanctuary. They had endured a violent ouster from Cloud Kingdom and a long, deadly slog through the jungle—they had no choice now but to fight.

Those who were with Bill—Luke, Omar, Maia, and Elena; his mother, Marisol; other friends and family; even the Elders—were tucked behind him, while Diego, the fierce and loyal Teddycat scout, stood by his side in a defensive stance, wielding his hefty walking stick.

Bill snarled and dug into the soft grass of Horizon Cove. His teeth and claws were bared. There was no telling how many creatures they would face. It had never been Bill's intention to fight anybody, from the humans to the crocs to whatever threat faced them now. But responsibility for the well-being of his loved ones landed squarely on Bill's young shoulders, and he had led the Teddycats to this place, promising safety and security. He couldn't allow anything to rip that promise away.

Slowly, the narrowed eyes drew closer, accompanied by a hissing sound. Bill's heart beat with a bruising force, and his muscles twitched in anticipation. He would have to rely on ancient jungle instincts to protect himself and the others, but surprisingly, he felt prepared. He had matured a great deal since leaving Cloud Kingdom. His shoulders were wider, his muscles fuller. The challenges of the journey through the jungle to Horizon Cove— clashing with humans, saying goodbye to good friends— had given Bill a renewed focus on what, and who, was truly important. While the old Bill might have panicked right about now, the new Bill felt no urge to flee. Deep down, he knew what his father would do. With any luck, someday he would tell Big Bill about the showdown over the future of Horizon Cove.

"Get ready!" Bill yelled. His eyes were hot and stinging with adrenaline. Everything was fuzzy in the pale darkness, clouding the corners of his vision. All around him the other Teddycats tensed their muscles and held their breath.

Diego leaned in. "What do you see, mate?"

"Whatever they are," said Bill, "there are a lot of them."

"More of us," said Diego, though Bill couldn't figure how the scout was so confident of that.

"We'll see," said Bill. He turned around. "Mom, you and Maia and Elena get the Elders and hide in the trees. I'll come for you all when it's safe. Luke and Omar, stay close to Diego and follow my lead."

"We're not going anywhere," said Marisol, resting a warm paw on her son's head.

"There's nowhere left to go," said Maia, pulling her sister closer.

The intruders inched into focus: crocodiles, long and studded with scales, their tails whipping back and forth. The Cove was a part of their hunting territory, and they welcomed the Teddycats' arrival with open jaws.

Bill's fur stood on end. He had faced the crocs before, but never on this scale.

"Well, here we go," said Diego, in a rousing, gravelly voice. "Long live the Teddycats!"

The crocs were nearly within striking distance when a loud squawking descended on the Cove. Bill and Diego looked up as a flock of bulky birds flooded the moonlit sky. The squawks rose to a piercing shriek as the bulky birds swooped down on the crocs, shielding the Teddycats with their wide wingspans and sharp beaks.

"What are these things?" Marisol cried.

The crocs seemed similarly flustered, angrily thrashing their tails and gnashing their teeth as the birds hopped up onto their heads and pecked at their eyes. The noise was almost unbearable as the birds' shrieking collided with the Teddycats' cries of panic, and Bill struggled to hold a plan in his head. The Teddycats had to take advantage of the birds' timely arrival and make a run for it! If they could make it to the tree line that beckoned from the back of the Cove, they could use their claws to climb to safety. But just as Bill turned to share his plan with the others, one of the birds scooped him up, lifting off the ground with a violent flutter of feathers.

"Hey, put me down!" Bill hollered.

The bird lifted further, dangling Bill from its claws. Bill jerked and flailed until he realized how high the bird had flown, and he watched as other Teddycats began getting plucked up by the birds. The biggest birds could carry three Teddycats at a time.

Bill could also see the crocs below him, clearly on the run and hustling back to the water, yelping in pain.

He spotted Maia and Elena in the clutches of one bird, his mother in another. The fear in their eyes was unmistakable. Bill was afraid too, but he realized that the birds—whatever they were—had saved the Teddycats from the crocodiles.

They flew higher, well above the trees. Had it been day, the view would have been striking. Bill wasn't scared of heights—after all, the Teddycats had once made their home in the clouds. But he had never been this high before. Dangling from a strange bird's talons was different from swinging from vine to vine. His hind legs kicked in the air as the talons dug into his chest.

The trees were far below, poking out of the darkness. He glanced up to get a better look at the bird, a sense of its intentions. But all he could see was the underside of the large, crooked beak. Below him, the rest of the Teddycats bellowed into the dark jungle as the birds carried them away from one danger but toward the terrifying unknown.